P9-BZW-860

THE
ARIZONA
CLAN

ZANE GREY

The
Arizona
Clan

WALTER J. BLACK, INC.

ROSLYN, NEW YORK

THE
ARIZONA
CLAN

THE
ARIZONA
CLAN

CHAPTER 1

Every day's ride added to Mercer's liking for this new country. He had placed so many days between the horizon-wide cattle ranges of Kansas and this vast upheaved Arizona land that he had forgotten the number. But he was sure it ran into weeks. Already he had to rake his memory to recall the dimming past. That seemed just as well. He was not particularly ashamed of it; he could look any man straight in the eyes, as straight as he had been compelled to shoot these last few hard years on the plains out of Kansas; but all the same, as it had seemed wise for him to ride far away into strange and lonely lands, so it was best to forget. At the back of Mercer's mind there had always been the belief that someday he would find the place meant for him, where his hazy dreams would come true. In his heart he knew he was not really the man the eastern ranges thought him.

All day his horse, Baldy, had jogged down a winding, rough road, seldom used, and where wheel tracks were dim. A heavy growth of pine had obstructed any extended view, although occasional rifts in the timber had permitted looking down into a magnificent blue-and-black valley beyond which loomed the jagged peaks of a mountain range. At length the pine failed for a growth of cedar and juniper, among which patches of manzanita gleamed red and stalks of mescal stood high out of the gray spiked plants. There were thickets of live oak and jack pine, and in the gullies sycamores and maples.

Above it had been a drowsy summer day; down here it was hot, and the blast of dry, fragrant air struck him as from a furnace. The forest was asleep. He saw more deer tracks than cattle tracks in the red dust along the road. Two days back a hunter had encountered him and told of the game down in this valley. What a change for Mercer to hunt deer and bear, instead of rustlers, instead of being hunted himself by drunken, notoriety-seeking range riders and cattle-town gunmen!

Baldy was tired and he limped, but he did not lag. Somewhere ahead there would be green grass and clear cold water. Mercer, too, was weary of the endless saddle seat during the day and saddle pillow all the long hours of the night. He was as hungry, too, as any grub-line rider who had ever ridden away from one cow camp toward another.

He was beginning to fear he would have to spend another night along the road. Somewhere down in this valley he ought soon to strike a ranch or a town or a sawmill, such as he had been informed was there. The road never ceased to wind, though it approached nearer a level. And presently, to his satisfaction, it turned to cross a wide rocky stream bed, in the middle of which a shallow rill of water ran. He was as keen to step into that clear water as was Baldy. He felt the cold through his hot boots. And he sprawled upon a hot, flat rock to drink his fill. What cold, wonderful, tasteless water! Baldy drank until Mercer was afraid he would burst. Then they waded out to the shade of the sycamores on the bank.

It was very pleasant here. The tinkle of the water was all the sound to disturb the forest serenity. Soon the sun would sink behind the mountain barrier in the west. Mercer wiped his sweaty face and thought of the hard biscuits and parched corn in his saddlebags.

Presently the silence broke to the click of an unshod hoof on stone. A man appeared around the turn of road leading a burro. As he drew near Mercer saw that he was a little old fellow, grizzled and stooped. The burro carried a water keg strapped on each side of a pack saddle. The man gave Mercer a sharp but not unfriendly look from narrow eyes.

"Howdy, stranger," he said crisply.

"How do," replied Mercer slowly.

"Hot an' dry, ain't it? This hyar country is shore burnin' up. Never seen the crick so low." And the old fellow proceeded to unstrap one of the kegs.

"My horse is frazzled out and so am I. Any place near where we can get lodging?"

"Wal, you're welcome to my shack," drawled the other. "But it ain't much, an' there's a good tavern at Ryeson."

"Thanks. I'll go on to Ryeson if it's not far."

"Less'n two mile."

"Good. I'm lucky today. What's this place Ryeson? Town, sawmill, or cow camp?"

"Wal, Ryeson's a tolerable big town. Fact is, it's the only one in the Tonto. There's two saloons besides the tavern. An' Sam Walker's store, an' the Timms Brothers' store, an' Hadley's blacksmith shop, an' the church, town hall, an' school all in one, an' I reckon a dozen or so houses, an'—"

"Quite a place," interrupted Mercer thoughtfully. "Any ranches?"

"Shore. Strung few an' far between all down the valley."

"That so? Surprises me. I wouldn't take this for a cattle country."

"Wal, cattle grow fat hyar when they're skin an' bones on the uplands. Water never fails, an' if the grass fails, as it has this summer, there's always browsin'!"

"You don't say. Interesting. I sort of like this country. Where do the cattlemen drive stock?"

"Maricopa. It's over the mountain range south, nigh two hundred miles."

"Whew! This is a wild country. What's here besides cattle?"

"Wal, there's Injuns, an' any amount of bars, cougars, turkeys, deer."

"I reckon I'll stop. But I meant what kind of work for a fellow besides riding?"

"Shucks of work, if you ain't pertickler aboot wages. Any handy man can get a job. Trouble hyar is none of the young bucks want work. Lots of bizness goin' on around Ryeson but little money movin'."

[4]

"Tell me where to get a job. I'd rather be far out of town."

"Wal, only the other day I heahed Rock Lilley roarin' aboot not havin' anyone to cut his sorghum."

"Sorghum? What's that?"

"Say, you never heahed of sorghum?" inquired the old fellow, with a bright gleam in his eyes.

"No, sir, I never did."

"Humph. An' I reckon then you never heahed of white mule, neither?"

"I got kicked by one once. You mean just an ordinary white mule?"

"Nope. This white mule ain't ordinary atall. He can kick like hell. . . . Wal, as I was sayin', Rock Lilley was roarin' cause none of his boys would stay home an' cut the sorghum. Rock's got six strappin' boys an' I don't know how many girls. They're shore a real old Texas family."

"What's Rock's business? Ranching?"

"Shore, he's got some cattle runnin' wild. Seldom drives to Maricopa. Kills a beef now an' then, or makes a trade. Hunts bar most of the time."

"How does he make a living then, let alone paying wages to a rider?"

"Haw! Haw! Thet's a stumper. I jest cain't tell you, stranger. Rock an' his family air pore, but they git along somehow. Jest had a purty dotter come home from some aunt or suthin' in Texas. I seen her an' wisht I was young once more."

"Damn! I'd better dodge that Lilley outfit!" exclaimed Mercer, discouraged. "How about some other cattleman?"

"Wal, you might try Simpson, across the valley from Lilley."

"What's he?"

"Same as Lilley. Only he ain't pore."

"Then he'd be the better man to hit for a job."

"Shore. But Simpson never hired no rider since I been hyar, ten years an' more."

"Ahuh. Big family same as Lilley?"

"Most as big."

"Reckon I was wrong about this being my lucky day," observed Mercer, as he arose. "Much obliged, old-timer. I'll be on my way."

He started off leading Baldy, meaning to walk for a while.

"Wal, so long, young fellar," called the old man. "Take keer you don't git kicked by thet thar white mule."

"Funny old geezer," soliloquized Mercer. "Wonder what that white mule is. Kind of a gag, I reckon."

The road followed the brook and wound under picturesque old sycamores and here and there a pine. Mercer peered through the trees trying to locate the old man's cabin, but was not successful. Trails straggled up from the brook to vanish in the forest.

While Mercer tramped along, the sun set and twilight descended magically. The air cooled perceptibly. He liked the mountain feel of it. And already the sweet, dry odor of the valley had intrigued him.

It was almost dark when the road led out into the open and he discovered that he had arrived at the village. Dark-colored houses, some with lights, lined each side of a wide square. He went on until he saw a group of people in front of what appeared to be a store. It had a high board front with undecipherable lettering. Horses stood in the dusk. He saw a buckboard and a wagon. The sound of low voices broke upon his keen ear.

Mercer was quick to sense the atmosphere. Well he knew frontier towns in the cool of a summer evening when the tranquillity seemed charged. He approached a boy on the outskirts of the crowd.

"Johnny, how about feed an' bed for my horse an' some for myself?"

"Yas, sir. I'll take you 'cross to the inn. Lemme lead yore hoss, sir," replied the youth eagerly.

"What's happened, boy?"

"Nuthin' much. Only Sim Perkins looked his last on white mule, so my pop says," replied the youngster, as he led Mercer across the wide square.

"His last look, huh? Must have got kicked pretty serious?"

"He's daid, mister. Thar was a game goin' on in Ryan's saloon, an' they got to shootin'. Some say Buck Hathaway did it. But Buck shore says he didn't."

"Little gunplay, eh? Is that common in these parts?"

"Enough to keep the population down, my pop says," replied the boy, with a laugh.

"Where's your sheriff?"

"Thar ain't none short of Maricopa. An' I never seen him, mister."

"Your Ryeson strikes me as an interesting town, Johnny. What's this white mule, anyway?"

[7]

"Wal, mister, if you don't know, I'm not tellin' you. Hyar's my pop's place. You go right in. Supper's ready, 'cause Ma rang the bell long ago. I'll look after yore hoss."

Mercer mounted a rickety porch and entered a dark hall at the back of which appeared to be a dimly lighted room. He went in slowly. Two men were eating at a long table. A woman entered from another door.

"Evening, ma'am. I'd like lodging for myself and horse."

"Jest git in, mister?" she asked sharply, and the searching look fitted her voice.

"This minute. Your boy met me."

"Set right down," she replied, more civilly. "I'll fetch yore supper."

Mercer took a seat opposite the men, whom he gave what might have been taken for a casual glance. The lamp cast a yellow glow on two hard faces that did not belong to cattlemen. They noticed where and how Mercer packed his gun before they looked at his face.

"Evening, men," said Mercer, as he sat down leisurely.

"Howdy, stranger," replied the older of the two.

Mercer felt a calculating curiosity but no particular antagonism in these individuals, and gathered from the meeting that strangers were not uncommon in Ryeson. The landlady brought his supper, and it was so hot and good that he would not have taken time to talk even if these men had been communicative, which they were not. They finished presently and stamped out. While Mercer was eating the boy returned, carrying his saddlebags and coat.

"I fetched yore things, mister," he said. "I'll put them in

hyar." And he pushed open a door in the middle of the room.

"How's my horse Baldy?" queried Mercer, when the boy came out.

"I'll bet it's long since he felt his oats. Fine hoss, mister. I looked after him good."

"Tom, whar's yore father?" called the woman from the kitchen.

"He's acrost the road."

"Wal, you run tell him to come git his supper, shootin' or no shootin'."

The youngster winked a bright eye at Mercer and thudded out into the dark hall. Mercer finished his meal, and rising went into the room for his coat. He thought he would wait until the boy's father came in. But as that event did not occur he went out to stand on the porch. There was more light along the square and more noise than before supper. Horses and people were moving. Some men passed and they were talking about the dry spell. He heard a woman laugh. Across the square he could see a number of people in a store that was brightly lighted.

He strolled over to make some purchases that his long ride had made necessary. The store was not like any other he had ever seen, although he could not at the moment define how or why. Still, it was a typical country store of general merchandise. While waiting to be served he studied the customers. His gaze encountered curious glances and at last the bold eyes of a handsome, audacious girl who entered with a companion. They giggled and talked of a dance, evidently to be held that night. Mercer had turned his back on many things, and one he hoped to dodge was trouble. Back on the Kansas and Panhandle ranges he had never been able to avoid it, though he had eternally tried, and had even earned the sobriquet "Dodge." He returned the buxom beauty's challenging gaze with one of sad appreciation and looked at her no more.

Finally he was waited on and carried his numerous parcels back to his room. A lamp had been placed at his disposal. Its wan light showed a bare room with a bed, a bench, and a washbasin, which, poor as they appeared, would be luxuries for him.

Mercer went out again and this time entered the nearest saloon. It at least possessed familiar attributes in the bar running full length, the gaudy mirror painted with suggestive figures, the haze of tobacco smoke, the smell of rum, the sound and sight of rough men. It had unusual merit for Mercer inasmuch as no one appeared to notice him. This was a relief, a comfort, an unfamiliar experience.

His intention was to purchase a good stiff drink, but the bar was crowded six deep by uncouth and grizzled men whom Mercer did not care to shove aside. Finding a box in a corner, he sat down to absorb the scene. There were long, lean, rangy riders present, bowlegged and red-faced and narrow-eyed. Their height struck Mercer, and they reminded him of Texas cowhands. This Arizona breed was certainly tall. But they might be Texans at that, for he had been told how much of the sparse population had come from the Lone Star State.

For the most part, however, the occupants of Ryan's saloon bore the earmarks of backwoodsmen. Some wore buckskin. Many of them were of mountaineer build, superb, full-chested, big-limbed, lacking wholly the characteristics of the range rider. Money did not appear to be lacking. There were several gambling games going on, one of poker, another of faro, and a third that was new to Mercer.

He forgot about his drink in his interest. The saloons of Hays City, Abilene, and Dodge, the notorious cattle towns he had frequented, lost by comparison with this one. They presented a stream of humanity drawn from every quarter—the parasites of the border and the cowhands they preyed upon. Here in Ryeson there was a much smaller, less noisy and wild, and apparently decent crowd. How easy to attribute much of that to the absence of the female hangers-on! Nevertheless, this Ryeson crowd seemed to possess the temper of flint, needing only the steel to draw fire.

Mercer watched and studied, got up to stand in the ring around the gamblers, and listened with all his ears, the upshot of which was a fund of thought-provoking perceptions and a store of mountain talk that fascinated and puzzled him. He left the saloon without having talked with anyone, and in doubt whether or not he wanted to linger in the valley town of Ryeson.

CHAPTER 2

Morning, however, found Dodge Mercer in a different mood. He decided he would not wander far from this valley.

He had breakfast early with the lad Tom and accompanied him to the barn to saddle Baldy.

"Air you ridin' on through, mister?" inquired the lad.

"Well, Tom, I reckon not, if I can find a job," replied Mercer.

"Aw, jobs air easy hyarabouts. You jest ride oot to Rock Lilley's an' hit him."

"Ahuh. An' why're you recommending him?"

"Wal, it's whar I'd go if I was big. I've hunted wild turkeys out thar. Wonderfullest place, jest between the Rock Rim an' the Bald Ridges."

"What else besides wild turkeys?"

"Laws, all kinds of game. An' peaches, watermelons, cabbage as big at thet, an' beans. Wait till you pile into a mess of beans Mrs. Lilley cooks!"

"Anything more, Tom? You got my mouth watering now."

"Wal, if I'm any judge of fellars you'd shore never pass up all that an' Nan Lilley, too."

"Ah, I see," replied Dodge casually. "Tom, here's a dollar. You're a boy after my own heart. And who's Nan Lilley?"

"Nan's one of old Rock's dotters," whispered Tom excitedly. "She's jest come back from Texas. I was too little when she went away. But she remembers me. Says she was fond of me. An', Mister, Nan's in a peck of trouble. I jest wisht you was a feller who'd follered her up from Texas."

Shrewd, bright, calculating eyes took stock of Mercer and somehow made him noncommittal.

"Trouble? Seems like I've heard that word somewhere. What's your girl friend's particular brand?"

"I don't know shore, mister. An' I'm scared to say what I think. But I'll take a chanct on you. I've a hunch Nan's trouble comes from white mule an' Buck Hathaway."

"One at a time, lad. What's this white mule?"

"You'll find out pronto. I'm not a squealer. But Buck Hathaway is the meanest fellar in this valley. He beats hosses an' kicks kids. He gambles an' he's a shooter, too, as everyone knows. The onliest thing he don't do is drink. Wal, Buck sort of took Nan Lilley to hisself, so they say. The fust dance after she got back he seen her an' he licked three fellars an' shot another—Jim Snecker, a cousin of mine. Crippled him. They say—these old wimmen hyar—that Nan is sweet on Buck. But I don't believe it. I seen Nan twice in town an' onct out to her home, in the woods, an' she cried an' cried. Ole Rock sets a heap o' store on Buck Hathaway. An' mebbe he means Nan fer Buck."

"Boy, how do you know Nan isn't sweet on Hathaway?" queried Dodge severely.

"Wal, I jest feel it. Don't you give me away, mister. I only had a hunch aboot you, too."

"Suppose you take me out to see her."

"Laws, I wisht I could. But I've gotta work. An' Pop's been drinkin'."

"How'll I find this Lilley ranch?"

"It's easy, mister, onct you're told. You cain't miss it. Take this road oot hyar—thet way—an' turn off fust road left. Go on till you come to the end. Thar's an ole log cabin an' two trails. Take the left agin an' keep on. It crosses the crick a lot of times, but you cain't miss findin' it. After a while you come to Rock's place."

"That's clear. But how'll I know your friend Nan?"

"Oh, lud, mister! You'd know *her* if you found her with a hundred gurls. She's jest lovely."

"All right, Tom, I'll take you up," replied Mercer, half-amused and half-earnest. "See you don't give *me* away."

"Laws, I won't never," rejoined the lad, his freckles standing out on his pale face and his eyes glowing. He hovered around Dodge while the saddle and bridle went on. And when Dodge mounted he concluded: "Ride oot the back way, mister. Folks is awful curious hyar. You kin hit the road by turnin' off where the pasture fence ends. Tell Nan I sent you."

Mercer bade the lad good-by and headed off as directed, making the road without having seen the town or any of its denizens by daylight. He had embarked on too many adventures not to recognize this as one. In any event, however, he would have called on both the Lilleys and the Hathaways before leaving the valley.

The morning was cool, with the air keen and sweet. Clear sky gave promise of another hot day. Colts were romping in a pasture and somewhere a burro let out his clarion blast. Mercer passed some cabins, and at length a ranch house back under a ridge pleasantly located amid corrals and fields. The sun had not yet topped the black-fringed plateau in the east. For the main part, however, Mercer could see only the black tips of dim mountains to the south and a level fringed black line of a lofty horizon-wide plateau to the north.

More ranches failed to materialize, although cattle trails led from the road on both sides. He concluded that what few ranches there were held to widely separated favorable levels in the valley. The sun soon came up, gold and hot, making away with the morning coolness. Flies and bees buzzed by. Some five miles or more from Ryeson came the first turn for Mercer, and it led to an old, rough, weedy road that had seldom felt a wagon wheel. It wound into the round oak-thicketed hills, and gradually climbed. Mercer welcomed the first pine tree. He loved trees because he had seen so few of them during his range riding. Those hills were dense with brush, cedar and piñon, and after a while the beautiful checker-barked junipers and more pines. All the foliage was dun-colored with dust. It had been many a week since rain had fallen on these low-lands. Every sandy wash between the hills was bone dry.

Now and then, when he looked back, he caught glimpses of the blue range to the south, and received the impression that he was getting high.

He passed a clearing that contained an ancient tumble-down log cabin of the most primitive make. It had a look that thrilled Mercer. What had happened there? Below this cabin was a rocky gully where mud-caked holes and myriads of cattle tracks proved that water ran here at some season. He climbed a long ascent through a forest of mixed timber, nothing large, though thickly matted. Rotting logs, leaves, and pine needles gave off an intoxicating odor, a woody tang, sweet and dry, and hot as the wind from a fire. Mercer inhaled deeply of that new and strange air. It seemed to exhilarate him.

When he gained the summit and turned into a bare hilltop he halted Baldy and gazed spellbound.

Rolling hills of green, like colossal waves of a slanted sea, rose to meet a black and red and gray mountain front, bold and wild, running from east to west as far as he could see, gashed by many canyons, with a magnificent broad belt of rock, gold in the sun, that zigzagged under the level, timber-fringed rim. This undoubtedly was what the lad Tom had called Rock Rim. Mercer reveled in the sight. How wonderful to a plainsman, whose eyes had grown seared with the monotony of the endless sun-blasted prairie! The air was still and hot. He heard the dreamy hum of falling water, and that seemed the only thing needed to make this wilderness scene perfect.

Then Mercer shifted his gaze and looked down more to his right than directly behind. And he was struck with amazement. He appeared to be high enough to look down upon a region of winding rounded ridges, like silver-backed, green-spotted snakes, between which yawned forest-choked gorges from which cliffs of bronze and crags of gray stood out. These ridges were miles long and they sloped down into a dark blue rent in the wildest cut-up bit of earth Mercer had ever looked upon. Beyond the bold, far wall of that canyon stood up a hummocky sea of domes and peaks, shaggy and black, remote and apparently inaccessible.

"Say, what have I hit on!" he ejaculated in delight. He had crossed the Rocky Mountains on horseback, but no colorful scene comparable to this had rewarded his searching sight. Mercer had to fight back the old reoccurrence of a boyish dream of the rainbow end. He had better not be too ecstatic.

Then, loath to leave, he rode on wonderingly. Soon he passed into the shade again, and that was welcome. He had begun a long slant down this high hill. It was getting on toward noon, which indicated that he had put many miles behind him. Soon the murmur of a tumbling stream filled his ears. The forest thickened, the trees grew higher, the shade darker. At length he reached the bottom of the slope to enter a wild clearing bright with golden flowers and colored sumach. A log cabin, with vacant gaping door, stood at the far end. To the left of this Mercer found the trail he was seeking.

It led down into the woods from whence came that drowsy, dreamy hum of a stream. Baldy felt the urge of the place and would have made short work of the remaining rough descent but for a strong hand on the bridle. Then the trail leveled across a sunlit shadow-barred glade to turn under great white-barked, green-leafed sycamores shading mossy boulders and a swift, amber-colored stream. No sign of drouth here! Mercer had left behind the hot, dusty, seared dry lands.

He got off to drink. The range rider's love of clear, cold water had been ingrained in him. And here it was satisfied to the utmost. He drank and drank, and gorged himself like a famished desert deer.

"Baldy, if we kill ourselves, we'll drink!" he ejaculated. "Snow water, or I'm a living sinner! To think of some of the stuff I've had to drink!"

He led Baldy across and sat on a boulder. The swift water had come up beyond his knees, and as if by magic had dispelled the heat of his person. Next to a horse he liked best a running stream. This one outdid even his dreams. It must head in some mountain fastness, perhaps that great tableland of which he had had a glimpse. Nature saw to it that there were inexhaustible supplies of water in rare and chosen wildernesses.

Mercer found the trail on that side and rode on, soon to ford the stream again. The trail followed it, and all the conditions that had made his introduction to this water-course so pleasant magnified as he journeyed on. Often he would rein in the contented horse to listen. The place seemed an endless solitude. No living creature crossed his path or gave sound to disturb the serenity. At length he ceased to count the times he had to ford the stream. And in truth such were the peace and beauty of the forest land,

and the ever-growing pleasure in the amber stream that he forgot his adventurous errand until his reverie was rudely disrupted by the distant bark of a hound.

This was a signal for Mercer to dismount and walk. After a few moments he smelled wood smoke, and it gave him poignant recollection of burning leaves and autumn in his boyhood. It was his intention to go directly to this mountain home of the Lilleys and introduce himself. But now that the time appeared close at hand he lagged somewhat, pondering in mind aspects of the situation that he had neglected to consider.

The stream brawled less and meandered more, as though reluctant to leave this cool, moss-bouldered mountainside for the rough, barren country below. Several times Mercer caught glimpses, through rifts in the trees, of hot gray ridges below. Probably the Lilley homestead nestled at the edge of the timber where this stream struck into the open.

Mercer came presently to the most beautiful spot he had ever seen. A bend of the stream encircled a bank an acre or more in extent, overcast by lofty pines and a marvelous silver-foliaged tree unfamiliar to him. Under these the wide-branched sycamores spread their contrasting limbs and leaves. A green-gold light appeared to swim in the drowsy summer air. Mercer left Baldy to nibble at a patch of grass and strolled on as if enchanted. Great rocks overhung the stream, all lichened in gray and russet and covered with lacy ferns and amber moss. In still, clear pools Mercer caught glimpses of huge trout lying motionless. This was almost the last straw. He crawled out on a rock as large and flat as a log cabin. A soft mat of pine needles covered it. Above stood out level spear-pointed branches of the silver-foliaged species of evergreen, unknown to him, and above that leaned the colored canopy of a great sycamore. It was a covert such as delighted his heart, at that moment returned to youthful pursuits, and he availed himself of the opportunity to spy upon the trout. But no sooner had he crawled to the desired position, feeling hidden and secure under the low-spreading branches, and certain of a sweet rest and watch there in the dreamy stillness of the summer-locked forest, when his keen ears, acutely attuned in this hour, caught a disturbing sound.

Mercer glanced up from the still, dark pool. A faint sigh came from the treetops, and it mingled with the soft tinkle and babble of the brook. A squirrel might have dislodged a pine cone. He listened, and at length caught a swishy sound, as of a body moving against brush. This came from the right of where he had been gazing and almost opposite him. He saw then that the trail led up a break in the cliff. A moment later a girl appeared with a wooden bucket swinging from her hand.

CHAPTER 3

Mercer gave a start. The girl was neither tall nor short. She walked with light step, though laggingly. When she came down out of the shade into a patch of softened sunlight he saw that she was bareheaded and barefooted. She passed behind a boulder to emerge out on the low rock ledge under which the water swirled, and kneeling she plunged the bucket into the stream and lifted it brimming full to set it down. The action disclosed a brown arm, round and strong, and supple shoulders.

She sat down on the moss, lifting her linsey skirt to dip her feet in the water. The distance across the stream to Mercer was scarcely thirty feet, yet she didn't see him. Indeed the great dark blue eyes, blankly tragic, appeared to note nothing there in the quiet woodland. Her face was youthful and clean-cut, too strong to be really what the lad Tom had so rapturously claimed, but it certainly had a strange and compelling beauty. Her hair was thick and clustering, of a chestnut hue where the sunlight caught gleams of gold. The quivering of red lips and the brimming of sad eyes acquainted Mercer with the prospect of being a spectator to grief. While he gazed, rapt and undecided, her expression slowly changed to one of acute distress.

That was the moment in which the rider realized he had at last, by many devious and hard ways, journeyed to the end of his rainbow. Wherefore he must not remain hidden there, a witness to grief not meant for curious and strange eyes.

"Howdy, Nan!" he called, almost gayly.

She heard distinctly, for her pretty head went up like that of a listening deer. Her face flashed brown as she turned it to left and right, while she hastily wiped her eyes. Mercer got the impression that she had been accosted thus before, there in the lonesomeness of her woods. Certainly she evinced neither surprise nor fear.

"Howdy, Nan," he repeated, just a little less boldly.

Suddenly she saw him.

"Howdy, yourself," she retorted.

Whereupon Mercer leisurely arose from his recumbent position, and spreading the foliage he sat down on the edge of the rock.

"I was watching the trout," he said frankly, smiling at her. "You came along to surprise me."

She took him in from his bare head to the spurs that jingled against the rock. Her look changed from speculation to astonishment.

"Are you sure you were watchin' only for trout?" she inquired with just a hint of doubt.

"Honest Injun."

"That trick has been played on me before, right here."

"I shouldn't wonder. But I give you my word I wasn't

looking for such good fortune. I left my horse grazing back a ways. I was dreaming along when all at once I saw the trout."

"Dreamin' along? You look it, mister," she said satirically.

"Thanks," he replied, as if he were complimented, and he smiled again at her. He saw how astonishment was leading to puzzled interest. If he could only prolong the interview!

"Who are you?" she queried, after a long pause.

"Do you mean my name—and what I am?"

"Both, I reckon."

"Mercer, John Mercer, but I've a nickname. Dodge! Funny, isn't it? Given me by pards because I was always dodging things."

"Dodgin' what things?" she went on curiously.

"Oh, everything, but mostly jobs, fights, bullets—and girls. I'm very shy of girls."

She let out a little peal of incredulous laughter.

"You look that, too. Where you from?"

"Kansas."

"Kansas!" she flashed, with excitement. "An' Dodge? That's where you got the name?"

"No. It was given me before I ever saw Dodge City."

"I came through Dodge on my way home from Texas. Oh, it sure was a terrible place. But Uncle Bill said it wasn't as bad then as before the railroad came."

"Say, did you travel alone all the way out here from Dodge?" asked Mercer severely.

"No. Uncle brought me. He's visitin' us. But I shore wouldn't have been afraid to come."

"You're a very brave girl for one so young."

"I'm eighteen years old," she rejoined spiritedly.

"You don't say? I reckoned you couldn't be hardly fifteen."

She eyed him dubiously, suddenly alive to her momentary laxity.

"Dodge Mercer, from Kansas?" she queried, returning to the issue.

"Yes, Miss. I was born in Pennsylvania. Ran away from school and home before I was fifteen. Became a cowhand in Kansas. Drifted west, and of late years have seen a lot of hard life on the Texas Panhandle and Kansas plains. I got sick of dodging so I hit out for Arizona. That's my story, Miss."

"You sure rode out of the fryin' pan into the fire. How'd you ever happen to drop into this Rock Rim country?"

"I just rode west. I see luck was with me."

"Luck? Sure, but it was bad. You better turn right around an' ride out of Arizona—leastaways, out of this Tonto Basin."

"After seeing you, Nan?"

"Yes, after seein' me, Nan!" she retorted pertly, while a little tinge of red showed in her brown cheeks.

"Is that advice, hunch, or threat?" he asked, in earnest good humor.

"Well, not a threat, but all the rest," she said soberly.

"Then I shall not ride away."

She had no ready answer for that, which plainly confused her for a moment. She glanced about at her bucket, and moved as if to rise, but she did not. The action, however, made her aware of her bare legs in the water half to her knees, and she hastily withdrew them and covered them.

"Nan, may I come over there and get acquainted with you?" went on Dodge directly.

"You're doin' pretty well on your side," she replied.

"It's so far I can't see what you look like," he complained.

"You'd get all wet. You can ride your horse over presently."

"Then you're going to ask me to your home?" queried Dodge eagerly.

"It's long past mornin' an' you're a long way from any ranch. My dad never lets any rider go by hungry or tired."

"Your dad? Oh, I see. You're not concerned about me starving or getting lost. Nan, this is the end of my journey."

"This? What do you mean? The woods—this brook—my dad's ranch—or what?"

"I reckon I mean you, Nan," he said.

If she was not offended she was surely nettled; still surprise and bewilderment had a share in her subtle change of demeanor. Dodge was swift to grasp that only sincerity could save him.

"Please do not take me as too forward with girls," he went on earnestly.

"How can I help it?" she asked incredulously. "Sure this is only Arizona backwoods an' I'm a poor backwoodsman's daughter."

"I am not playing. I couldn't be any more respectful if you were the daughter of the richest rancher in Arizona. But I don't want to wait a day or a week or a month to tell you things. Please let me come over there by you, Nan."

"How'd you know I was Nan Lilley?" she asked suddenly.

"I knew it when I saw you."

"How did you?"

"That lad at Ryeson—Tom, who took me to his home—he told me."

"Tommy Barnes?" she cried, her face relaxing. "The little rascal! When did you see him?"

"Last night. I rode in after dark. I met him and asked for lodging. He took me to his home. I told him I was looking for a job. He said I could get one at Rock Lilley's. This morning he was hoping I might be a Texas beau of yours, who'd followed you home. The lad was so keen, so eager, he seemed so fond of you, so anxious about you. Then he went on to say you were in trouble—that there was some mixup between your dad and a certain Buck Hathaway—that Hathaway was courting you and had your dad's favor —and last, that your trouble was you did not love this Buck Hathaway."

Her face flamed scarlet and she cried out: "The meddlin' little fool! To tell that to a stranger!"

"Well, his heart picked the right stranger, Nan. Now, can I come over there, so we won't have to yell at each other?"

"No! No! Oh, this is sure shameful," she cried, hiding her face in her hands.

Dodge waited a long, tumultuous moment. He had been abrupt, but what other explanation could he have offered? The truth was best. If Tommy had indeed been a little fool and if Nan really cared for this redoubtable Hathaway, then the sooner Dodge knew the better, and he could ride away as he had come. But his heart beat high and thick in his breast.

"Nan, if there's anything shameful in this you'll have to tell me, for I can't see it," he said finally.

"But I don't know you," she almost sobbed.

"I'll do my best to correct that. Let me come over there, unless, of course—" but he did not conclude that supposition. He waited until her composure returned, and she lifted her head, to look at him somehow differently.

"Why did you—come out—here?" she asked haltingly.

"I asked questions first because I needed a job. I would have come out to see your dad in any case. But to be fair and square with you, I've got to confess I took Tom's story seriously, and I came to get you out of your trouble."

She stared at him with darkening eyes that stirred his heart. If he had not fallen in love with Nan Lilley before he ever saw her he surely was doing it now. Excitement, however, and his whirling thoughts, and her sweet, disturbing presence obviated any possibility of self-interrogation then.

"You came out here to get me out of trouble?" she called across the stream in a high, sweet voice. Surely no one ever before had offered to help Nan Lilley. If it had not been for doubt and misgiving in her face and words she would have appeared overcome. "Mister Mercer, I'm not sure about you. It's too sudden—too—too— Why, if it were so, I'd—I'd bless you. But it can't be so because it can't be done."

"Why can't it? Of course I don't know what your trouble is. Was your little friend Tom telling me the truth?"

It struck Dodge that her eyes were trying to pierce a supposed disguise about him. She got up and stepped off the ledge from boulder to boulder until she was directly across from him and considerably nearer. She made a most charming picture, despite the suggestion of a forlorn soul struggling in her. Moreover, the perspective he got of her was a true one, and it thrilled him. The water swirled over her feet and up around her shapely ankles; she had forgotten restraint in her curiosity, and her graceful form poised tense, instinct with life; she held her arms outspread to keep her balance, and this accentuated the swelling curve of breast and neck. Dodge got to his feet. It was high time that he rode away from this secluded stream and alluring girl, unless by her own word or act she detained him.

"Go back," he said abruptly.

"I won't fall in. An' what if I did? Every day this hot spell I've walked in here—clothes an' all," she replied, with the first smile she had given him. It was an exhilarating magic.

"You might slip and strike your head."

"My poor head's empty, so it wouldn't matter."

"Nan, you've got the same devil in you that's in all women. Listen. Was Tom telling me the truth?"

"How could I admit it if he had—to you—when I only

saw you two minutes ago?" she asked, in helpless resentment.

"It looks like you're holding out your arms to me," he rejoined curtly.

Then she laughed outright. "Sure it does. But I'm not. Only balancin'."

"You've got me off my balance, too," he retorted. "Nan, this won't do. If you've intelligence and sense enough to grasp a real friend in me, all right. Only you'd better say so quick, or I'll ride away."

"I haven't any sense or intelligence or—or anythin'," she replied.

"Well, I don't believe you're talking as straight as I am. Girls can't be honest."

"I can. But you sure expect a lot on short notice."

"Either I stay or ride away. So what's the use of this long-acquaintance excuse?"

Dodge knew he must not linger there, unless she surrendered something that it seemed absurd to hope for. Still, she was on the defensive; she had not given in to the idea of his championship; she had not been roused to earnestness. All of which seemed to prove the futility of his case.

"Then I'm afraid you'll have to ride away," she replied demurely. Did she imagine that he would not? What hid in the deep shadows of her eyes?

"You can settle that quick," he replied ringingly. "But you'll need to excuse a question that no stranger has a right to ask on first sight. All the same, I'll ask it. Do you love this Buck Hathaway?"

Her breast heaved. A flash of dark passion crossed her face. "I hate him!" she cried.

Then they gazed long into each other's eyes across the stream.

"Thank you," replied Dodge presently. "That confidence is more than I deserved—or expected. I will not ride away. Suppose you go back on the bank. I'll come over."

"But you'll get all wet," she returned dubiously.

Dodge felt there was no help for him. The reaction of relief, owing to her passionate repudiation of Hathaway, led to a conflict of emotions. He was about to drop off the rock when she said: "I'll come over. We can hide under the branches. Some of the kids may come whoopin' here any minute."

She lifted her skirt above her knees as she stepped down into the water. That was an enchanting moment for Dodge and if it had been needed, his utter subjugation would have begun right there. The golden, dark-barred sunlight seemed to whirl above him; the stream murmured on in its infinite solitude, as if to assure him there were no other eyes than his to see Nan Lilley wade the pool. She moved boldly, surely, sometimes with a long step from one deeply submerged rock to another. Dodge gazed down upon her rippling hair, her pensive face bent as she peered for places to step, and he could not believe his eyes. The miraculous was happening. Someone was coming to meet him. He swore in his heart that it would never be anything for her to regret.

Then she uttered a wild little cry and leaping like a

nimble goat she gained a stone on the bank below, and let her skirts fall.

Dodge leaned down with outstretched hands. She was off her balance, but caught it in time, and thus supported she sprang up beside him. He spread wide the branching foliage to admit her into the secluded leafy nook and let it swing back.

"You found my hidin' place," she said wonderingly. "Strange! It's all strange—this meetin', an' all about you. I used to come here when I was a little girl—hundreds of times—an' I've been here often since I came home."

Mercer had kept one of her hands, despite gentle efforts on her part to release it. And he still held it as they sat down, both obsessed with the idea of looking at each other. She gained from close observance. He laughed inwardly at a wild desire to kiss the red curved lips. Her eyes appraised him, beautiful in solemn, penetrating strength.

"What do you take me for, anyhow?" she queried suddenly, indicating by a glance her hand imprisoned in his.

"I reckon I'm proving that," he answered simply.

"You're a bold fellow—or maybe bad," she mused.

"I wasn't much good back there on the Kansas ranges," he admitted. "All I can ask now is that you give me the benefit of a doubt and wait."

"Wait for what?"

"Till I can prove what I'd like you to know."

"And meanwhile you'll hold my hand, kiss me, hug me, and all the rest?" she queried, halfway between doubt and scorn.

"Have I offended you?" he asked gently.

"No, and that bothers me. Is it in you or me? Oh, I've been run after by most of the boys in this valley. I know them. I've kept them off, except Buck Hathaway, who fights me for kisses. I can't trust him or any of them."

"Please don't class me with them," he said stiffly. "You observe that I haven't attempted any liberties."

"You won't let go my hand," she protested.

"Are you making any violent effort to get it away?" he asked.

She was not, and she knew it. Evidently she felt in a quandary, though quite self-possessed. It was inexpressibly sweet for Mercer to realize that his presence swayed her, that she wanted to trust him, that there was something fine and moving and fateful in this meeting.

"You are different. And Tommy sent you. But—but—"

"Nan," he interrupted, "I think it was when you came down the trail that I fell in love with you. If not then, surely when you waded the stream to come to me."

"Nonsense!" she cried, blushing scarlet. Nevertheless, instead of being nonsense it was something tremendous, that seemed to exercise an irresistible power to agitate her.

"Don't you believe in love at first sight?" he asked.

"I—I don't know. But here, I mustn't let you make love—"

"Nan Lilley, you're no stranger to me. This hour has been like a year. I was ripe for this adventure. When I tell you my story you'll believe then that our meeting wasn't just accident."

"Then tell me," she said eagerly.

"Sometime. What I want to get at now is this. Give me time to prove I'm to be trusted. And that's asking you to marry me then, Nan."

"Marry you!" she cried, in shame and amaze. "Why, man, my dad has pledged me to Buck Hathaway."

Mercer in a passion of dismay released her hand and snatched her in his arms. But before he had yielded further to such impulse she braced a strong hand against his breast and held herself back. Still, her face was dangerously close.

"There you go," she whispered. "Takin' my breath." She seemed startled at losing poise, and for the moment imminently near catastrophe.

Mercer took it that the catastrophe would be his falling to the status of these backwoods louts she scorned, and he gave stern rein to his impulses. He let her push herself slowly back to the length of her arm, and there they sat for a space, her hand spread on his breast, her eyes, darkly dilated, fixed on his, as if irresistibly fascinated, and waiting for she knew not what.

"There! That ought to prove I love you," he said, breathing hard, and let her choose whether he meant his passionate clasp or his equally passionate restraint. Not until he fully released her, a moment later, did he divine that he might have dared further. "You surprised me, Nan. I hope you'll forgive that. After all my bragging I fell down! But you are what Tommy said. I've gone a long way since I first set eyes on you."

Probably she took his admissions for resignation, for the startled expectation died out of her face. She sank back lax. Little flecks of sunlight filtered through the leaves to brighten her hair. The wet skirt clung to her round limbs and the water ran from it to float pine needles in little pools. She seemed the very breath of the woodland and a cool, subtle allure emanated from her. Mercer thought of the strangeness of them sitting there in this foliage-screened covert. There was no denying it. And the fact was incalculably significant. He did not need to have her tell him that she would meet him there again, even if she realized it. But he knew, and he was not concerned with the strong attraction of such possibility but the right or wrong of it.

"You'll go away now?" she queried at length.

"Do you think I ought to?"

"I reckon you had."

"Do you *want* me to go?"

"I can't say I do."

"Then I'll stay."

"But that'd be wrong. My dad is head of the Lilley clan. We have no law except his word. Somehow the Hathaways can work him to their wishes. They're gettin' our cattle, our horses, and now they'll soon get me. If you stay here I—I'll be worse off. Because I'll be sure to—to like you, to want to be with you—to—to— Oh, it'll just happen! And that'd be wrong."

"No. It'd be right. The wrong would be for you to let your dad force you to be Hathaway's wife. If you don't love him, it'll be wrong to marry him."

"Yes. But then it only falls on my head," she replied mournfully.

"Nan, you're sacrificing yourself," he said, suddenly keen again. "This, then, is your trouble?"

"The littler part because it only concerns me. The big trouble is that since I've been home I've found out terrible things, and they're breakin' my heart. Dad has cancer and can't live long. My brothers are drinkin', idlin', while we're gettin' poorer. The Hathaways have a lien on our land. We owe a year's debt to Timms' store for supplies, my mother is failin'—and, oh, Mister Mercer, us Lilleys are goin' to hell!"

"Suppose you call me Dodge from now on when we're alone," he said eloquently.

"Call you Dodge? Is that the—the way you take my confidence?"

"Yes. Back on the plains I earned that name," he replied. "I never dodged trouble in all the ten years I rode the range. I never dodged a night's watch, or a stampede of stock, or a rustling outfit, or cards, or gamblers, or women, or fights, or bullets—nor dealing death. That's why they called me Dodge. I rode away at last because I wanted to dodge all those damned things—to find a new life among new faces where there wasn't any trouble. But I guess there's no such place on earth. I rode a thousand miles or more to run into you and your trouble—which I shall make mine. Now suppose you call me Dodge, just for the fun of it. To see how it sounds from you."

"*Dodge!*" she burst out, swayed by his impassioned speech.

"Say! It sounds powerful appealing from you, Nan. Sort

of fits when you say it. But I reckon you better not say it again here."

He arose, and offered his hand to help her up. "Now let's go tackle your troubles. That about your dad having cancer is bad, but the rest don't faze me."

"Oh, you make me hope!" she cried. "You make me want to fight! I—I don't care—I'm glad you came. I prayed, oh, I prayed!"

"Well, I don't know if I was ever an answer to prayers," he drawled, smiling down upon her. "But anything might happen. I'll go get my horse, Baldy."

Dodge emerged from the green covert out into the open of sun and shade, and he walked back on the trail as one in a dream. The forest land seemed to wrap him in its warm, fragrant breath; the tall pines sang and the stream murmured on; the solitude found the soul in him that had ever struggled to rise. Whatever befell him there could only leave him better, and he embraced the adventure. He would befriend this little backwoods girl irrespective of any thought of himself.

He found Baldy where he had left him, and mounting he rode back on the trail, which swerved to the left of the rocks where he had encountered Nan. Suddenly he saw her across the stream, waiting for him. Baldy halted in the middle of the wide shallow where the trail crossed and drank like the desert horse that, thirsty or not, would never be turned from pure, cold water. While he drank Mercer looked at Nan. At that distance her dark, deep eyes held a watchful observance.

Soon he joined her on the bank and dismounted.

"What a horse! Baldy, you called him. All for that white face!"

For reply Dodge put his hands under Nan's arms and in a single heave lifted her to a side seat in the saddle.

"I'll carry your bucket," he said, with a laugh. "We'll make an effective approach. I hope Hathaway is there to see us."

She eyed him ponderingly, unconscious of her betrayal of mingled admiration and misgiving.

"I reckon you're a devil," she replied thoughtfully. "But you're sure not goin' to see me fall down. When we get there I'll introduce you as—as a friend from Kansas."

"Taking a hunch from Tommy?" he inquired gayly.

"It might be a good one, though it'll sure upset the Lilleys."

"Then I'm supposed to have met you in Kansas, say at Dodge City—followed you out here?"

She gazed down upon him with wonderful, thought-provoking eyes. "On your head be it, Dodge."

He picked up the bucket and started up the trail leading Baldy. Once up on the bank he found that the edge of the forest was near, and that a blue-and-gray space appeared to yawn beneath. He saw a long, low, dark log cabin just below the line of pines. Evidently the stream ran to the right of it.

When Mercer walked out of the woods he was confronted by a great cleared space, rich in green growths, slanting down to where the timber showed dark and ragged again. Beyond was such a magnificent vista of rugged, uneven, colorful valley that he was spellbound.

He was looking down upon the bare silver ridges and brush-choked gorges which he had seen from the hilltop some miles to the west, only here, right upon them, as it appeared, the effect was incalculably magnified. Miles of a great, black, shaggy canyon fronted the left wall of the wilderness, and into it all these gorges and ridges fell. The glory and the beauty of the mountain forest land lay all behind him, under the bold Rock Rim. Below stretched a harsh grandeur, a ghastly gashed world the like of which he had never seen before.

He had only time for a glance when a pack of savage hounds burst from under the peach and apple trees that partly obscured the cabin.

"Here, you wild dogs!" called Nan. "Get back! You, Sounder! Here, Moze, Tige, behave yourselves."

The chorus of bays and barks ceased, and the long-eared hounds trotted to and fro, wagging their tails, but eying Dodge distrustfully. He followed the path, to emerge into a grassy plot before a most picturesque old log cabin, backed by the towering pines, and open all its long-porched front to view of the valley below.

"Here we are," said Nan, cool and sweet, as Dodge halted before the wide steps that led up to the high porch. Dogs and children peeped out from under the porch rail. He heard a clink of spurs, a deep voice. He saw the peak of a black sombrero. "Dad, Uncle Bill, Ma—all of you come out here an' meet my friend from Kansas."

Nan, sitting on Baldy, could see up on the porch, while Dodge was too low. She was gay and audacious, and if the occasion was momentous she had the nerve to meet it. A heavy footfall sounded on the porch.

"Wal, friend of Nan's, come up an' show yourself," called a hearty voice that held a ring Dodge trusted.

"Go up, Dodge, and run the gantlet. It's what you get for chasin' after me way out here."

Dodge would have faced fire or a den of lions for the thrilling and unexpected attitude of the girl in what surely must be a trying if not desperate situation. He mounted the steps, and setting the bucket down he looked up. A superb, craggy-faced man of about fifty years stood there, the black sombrero Dodge had espied from below cocked back on his shaggy, grizzled head. His visage was a remarkable one, and Dodge needed only one look into it to realize that he was safe here. Piercing hazel eyes with dancing flecks that caught the sunlight looked him up and down. He had beetling brows, high cheekbones under which his cheeks sunk in, and a rugged, scantily bearded chin.

"Dad," called Nan from the saddle, "meet my friend from Kansas—Dodge Mercer. Dodge, that's my father, Rock Lilley."

"Glad to meet you, sir," said Dodge, extending his hand.

"Same to you, young man," was the robust reply, and then Mercer's gun hand was subjected to a squeeze that was not good for it.

"Mercer? Ain't thet name familiar? Whar'd I hear it, Bill?" queried the mountaineer.

"And Dodge," called up Nan roguishly, "that hard-lookin' Texas hombre is my Uncle Bill Lilley."

This individual emerged from behind Lilley, and Nan's good-humored epithet was felicitous. Texas was written all over that stalwart uncle, and if Dodge had needed a friend he would have wished it to be he. If Dodge could judge men, here was the salt of the earth.

"How do, Uncle Bill Lilley," said Dodge.

"Dodge Mercer, huh, late of Abilene?" drawled the Texan.

"Oh, Lord, it's a small world. I reckoned Arizona was far away," ejaculated Dodge plaintively.

Nan called out again, this time nervously: "Ma, come on out. Sally, Rose, and you boys, where's your manners?"

Dodge noticed several womenfolk at the back of the porch, where there appeared to be a wide space between two parts of the cabin, both of which were under one wide, shelving roof. He saw some lean, long, still-faced, still-eyed young men who lounged motionless.

"Wal, it shore is a small world," spoke up Uncle Bill. "Dodge, I was in Abilene last April, with my last trail herd. I saw yore meetin' with Strickland."

Dodge's heart sank. Of all the miserable luck! His past could never be effaced. It would follow him everywhere. His mute gesture of poignant regret was misunderstood by the Texan.

"Wal, I shore know how you feel," he drawled. "But you needn't apologize for thet little gunplay. Strickland was a big man in Abilene. But I've heahed more'n one say you did the community a service. Thet's the frontier, Mercer. We cattlemen could never have made out but for you handy boys."

"Thanks. It's good of you to take that angle," replied Dodge, fighting the cold sickness of an old mood. "I got tired being hounded by Strickland's friends. So I hit out for the West. I'm sure glad to meet you all, but sorry I just couldn't have been plain nobody."

"Haw! Haw! Thet cain't be, son," declared Uncle Bill lustily, and he turned to his brother. "Rock, wasn't it only the other day thet I mentioned Mercer's name to you, along with some others well known in the cattle towns?"

"Shore. I remembered when Nan spoke, an' I was plumb surprised."

"Wal, I reckon it's no bad news for us thet Nan's friend happens to be from the Kansas and Panhandle country, an' shore the same breed as King Fisher, Wild Bill, Wess Hardin', an' some more of them gun-throwin' gents."

"Hell no! Whar's thet jug?" roared Rock Lilley.

Uncle Bill turned to the bench where he had been sitting and upon which sat a queer little brown jug. He tipped it with one hand, his thumb in the ring.

"To all friends of Texans," he called out. Then he drank and lowered the jug. "Aagh!" His face was purple.

Rock Lilley took the jug and imbibed with no expression save a singular smacking of his lips. Whereupon he handed the vessel to Mercer.

"Look out, Dodge," trilled Nan, her voice troubled. "You're goin' to be kicked."

But Mercer, happy at the turn of his introduction there, felt prepared for anything.

"To new friends," he said, and took a swift pull at the jug. Something happened. A terrific shock, a vitriolic burn, a sudden blindness assailed him simultaneously. A torturing fire seemed to move slowly down inside him and to explode. The impact of searing bullets had done less to him.

"My—God!" he gasped, as he staggered to set down the jug. "What was—that stuff?"

"Haw! Haw! Haw!" laughed the Lilleys in unison.

Nan appeared hazily in Dodge's returning sight. "I warned you, Dodge," she said.

Rock Lilley stretched out a long arm to slap a heavy hand on Dodge's shoulder.

"Son, thet was Arizona white mule!"

CHAPTER 4

Never had a short succession of days been packed so full of pleasant incident and toil as those few following Mercer's establishment at Rock Lilley's ranch. From the head of the clan to the smallest tot, Dodge had received more than was due the stranger within the gates. Uncle Bill and little Rock, the twin brother of little Rill, took especially to the Kansas rider. Nan's aloofness, her watching observance, augured so well for Dodge's cause that he dared not press it.

Saturday had come, a midsummer day, and with Uncle Bill, and Steve, the oldest Lilley boy, a man in stature and mood if not in years, Dodge was in the thick of sorghum cutting.

"Doggone! I don't know what's come over me," he said to himself. But he knew well enough, if he would have admitted it. For a young man who had been a cowhand for years, initiated into a breed that seldom departed from the use of saddle, rope, and gun, he had assuredly taken up mountain labor with astounding vim. But what a relief to get free of the old irksome, monotonous duties!

The day was hot and his clothes were soon wringing wet. The musty odor of the sorghum was not unpleasant, the rustle and patter and crack of the ripe stalks delighted his ears; always the great gold-barred, black-fringed rim towered above him, crowned by blue sky and white clouds. When he paused to wipe the sweat from his face he also glanced over at the top porch of the log cabin, where now and then he would see Nan watching him. The sunlight shone on her hair. At these moments his heart sang, and untoward thoughts, presages of future strife, would not abide with him. The shadow that hovered over the Lilleys seemed less tangible.

Just to be there, to work, to feel these backwoods Lilleys coming to like him, to see Nan at intervals, to realize that whatever had enticed him to the valley was inevitable—these things aroused in Mercer a closer approach to happiness than he had known for years. And it meant so much that he dreaded close penetration of the Lilley household, and likewise introspection of his own peculiar state.

At noon the toilers rested under a dense juniper that had been spared by the pioneer. Sammy and little Rock fetched the noonday food and drink. And that was a pleasing hour for Mercer. Mostly he had listened, but questions multiplied behind his lips.

Little Rock manifested his usual curiosity about Dodge, and he was not yet old enough to be affected by the mountain shyness.

"What fer you pack thet when you work?" he asked, pointing at Dodge's gun.

"Rock, I wouldn't feel dressed if I didn't wear that."

"You're a funny fellar. Sammy, he says it's the same as his pants."

"Lad, thet's a habit of Texans and cowmen back in a country not so good to live in as this," replied Uncle Bill.

"Tell us aboot it, Uncle Bill," they implored, and in the end it was Dodge who had to enrapture them with a wild story. At length, barefooted and tousle-headed, the youngsters took up the empty pails and skipped away. Steve picked up his cutter and returned to work.

"Uncle Bill, have you noticed anything queer about this field of sorghum?" asked Dodge, at length launching a query that had tormented him.

"Wal, now, hev you?" countered the Texan evasively.

"Sure have. Every morning some shocks we stacked are missing. I wasn't certain till the third day I'd worked. I've looked all over but I can't find track of them. Now, where'n hell did those stacks go?"

"Wal, son, fer a Panhandle rider you shore ain't observin'," drawled the other gruffly.

"I just took a look around," replied Dodge, to excuse himself. There seemed to be satire or rebuke in Lilley's remark.

"A hoss man looks fer tracks. Air you any good at trailin'?"

"Don't rub it in, Uncle Bill. I have trailed unshod horses over rocky country. But here I hadn't reckoned it enough of my business."

"Natural. But you cain't escape it here. I've bin waitin' to talk about this outfit an' what they're up agin. You never 'peared serious aboot it."

[45]

"Serious? Say, Uncle Bill, I reckon I'd never admit how serious I am," replied Dodge quickly.

"Wal, you better git serious damn good an' pronto."

"Very well, old-timer. Shoot!" retorted Dodge, as if throwing off a mask. He had nothing to hide and all to gain. Moreover, Texans of this ilk had always had his profoundest respect.

"Wal, you ain't so slow, after all," replied Lilley, with a grin. "I reckon you kin move some when you git goin'. This heah sorghum crop 'pears to interest you. Do you know what it's used fer?"

"I hadn't thought much about that, Uncle Bill. I supposed for grain and fodder. That's why I was surprised not to find those missing shocks stowed away in the barn."

"Grain an' fodder yore eye!" snorted the old Texan. "It's growed fer nothin' but moonshine whisky."

"What?" flashed Dodge.

"Moonshine, I said. Or in Arizonie lingo—white mule."

"Well, I'll be damned!"

"Son, I had a hunch thet one swig of white mule was enough fer you."

"I just guess yes. Unless I'm forced, as in another instance like that one. Then believe me I'd be thundering careful not to swallow too much at one gulp. It'd kill me."

"Dodge, I shore couldn't ask no more fer you or Nan," rejoined the Texan feelingly.

"Nan!" ejaculated Dodge, startled.

"Don't jump oot of yore boots," replied Lilley imperturbably. "I reckon I said Nan."

"Aw, old-timer, don't say *she* ever did or ever would drink that stuff?" implored Dodge.

"Hell, no! I meant it was good fer Nan thet you couldn't see white mule."

"Yes, of course, Uncle Bill. I—I—maybe I understand. But what's my not drinking got to do with her?"

"Son, come clean an' straight as you shoot," demanded the Texan.

"Uncle Bill, you've got the drop on me. I swear to God, I'll be as clean and straight with Nan Lilley as you could want me."

"Wal, I'm thankin' heaven you rode along," replied Lilley fervently, a horny hand on Dodge's. "We'll talk agin whar we kin be alone. Steve oot thar is watchin' us. Only this, Dodge. Git to thinkin'. You're too happy to use yore haid. An' heah's somethin' to think aboot. Nan is in a tight fix heah. She hates young Hathaway, fer which I shore don't blame her. No use fer us beatin' aboot the bush! No more'n the use to talk to my brother. You'll hev to kill Buck Hathaway. Howsomever, thet's nothin' fer Dodge Mercer. Heah's a lot wuss. It's white mule thet's burnin' up the Lilleys."

"*White mule!*"

"Nuthin' else, an' nuthin' else could be so shore an' bad. Pore old Rock thinks he's got cancer. But it's white mule thet's dragged him to debt an' ruin, an' will be his death. Too late fer us to save Rock! But we shore kin save Nan, an' mebbe the boys."

"Bill, I always liked you Texans," replied Dodge, and

[47]

that was his answer to the dark and piercing light in Lilley's glance.

"Wal, let's git back to work," rejoined the other.

That was the end of Dodge's pleasant daydreams. At once a somber thoughtfulness pervaded his consciousness. Indeed he had been blind to the handwriting on the wall. The shadow he had vaguely perceived stood out in all its appalling suggestiveness. The secret of Rock Lilley's idle, jovial hours stood revealed—his occasional vacancy of eye, his cough, his nocturnal habits, his periods of terrible brooding, his ghastly pallor and his dusky flush, the subterranean rumblings from his deep chest. Six stalwart sons, but only one of whom would work! Perhaps their frequent long absences from home and the stealthy removal of the sorghum by night meant that they had a moonshine still hidden in one of the canyons. The trouble in Nan's eyes and the havoc in the face of the breaking mother—Dodge well understood them now. And the thing loomed forebodingly. The mother knew the full truth, but Nan only surmised it.

The afternoon passed with Dodge unmindful of the fleeting hours. A great swath he had cut in the yellowing sorghum attested to his unconscious labor. He toiled on after Uncle Bill and Steve had gone. And the sun was sinking behind the gold-rimmed promontories when he wearily plodded back to the cabins.

Was it the same? Nan waved a furtive hand from the upper porch, but that evidence of a secret rapport between them failed to thrill him. The hounds bayed, the children chattered, the fragrant blue smoke circled against the dark pines, the last rays of sunset streaked through the lilac haze, the stream murmured on, and the sweet sough of wind sang in the treetops. But these failed to affect Dodge Mercer this momentous day. Nor did he listen to Rock Lilley's noisy welcome from the porch. Over the seeming peace and tranquillity of that homestead hung a menace.

Dodge washed away the toil stains and carefully picked his way up the porch steps, encumbered with Sammy and little Rock and Rill, who clung to his boot straps and gun sheath. The long table, placed between the two cabins, was laden with food. Two long benches afforded seats for the large family, and the big, crude chair was set in state at the end for the chief of the Lilley clan.

Nan helped Sally and Rose wait on the table until all were served, then they took their respective seats, which, however, never appeared to be the same. This night Nan sat across from Dodge and he was not slow to catch her apprehensive look. His return glance might have said much, but it was not smiling.

After supper Dodge sat on the porch steps, and when the melancholy dusk settled down and the cool air replaced the sultry, Nan slipped to a seat beside him.

"What's the matter, Dodge?" she whispered.

"I'm tired an' blue, sweetheart," he replied, in a low voice.

She caught her breath. Since the day of their meeting he had never uttered a word that might encroach upon the rights of the accepted suitor, Buck Hathaway. That he did so now augured some subtle change.

"Don't let anyone hear you say that," she begged.

"Not even you?"

"Dodge, you're different tonight."

"Well, I reckon. The world seems different. But I'll cheer up soon."

"How soon? It scares me for you to be gloomy."

"Nan, you remember you told me about tapping on the log that runs up by the porch roof? How your favorite brother Steve used to sleep up there, under the corner eaves, where my bed is now? How you, sleeping in the room below with the kids, used to signal to him?"

"Sure, I remember," she said.

"Well, I'm thinking it'd be something to do for me. My pillow lies right against that log. I could hear the lightest tap. So suppose we make up signals?"

"It'd be fun, if—if you think it's all right. What signals, for instance?" she added dubiously.

"Let's see," he drawled coolly, and tapped the step. "One, like that, means good night. . . . Two, like that, means pray for me. . . . And three, like this—I love you! . . . Don't ever forget to listen."

"Dodge, can you talk so—so crazy—when tomorrow is Sunday and Buck Hathaway will be here?"

"Nan, your father gave me a job and a home on one condition—that I would respect his pledging of you to Hathaway. I could see what his word meant to him. Once given, it could never be broken. That is his creed. Well, I accepted. I meant to live up to it. But something has happened which makes me break my promise. I shall never give you up to Hathaway."

"Oh, Dodge! You terrify—me," she whispered.

"Is that all?"

"It fills me with shame."

"No more?"

"Oh, I can't tell you. A wild, sweet gladness! Dodge, please don't make—love to me."

"Why not?" he asked recklessly, and then as heavy footsteps sounded on the porch he whispered in her ear not to forget to listen for the tapping signals on the log.

At dark the children were put to bed. The men sat in the darkness on the porch, smoking. They talked of casual things, relating to the ranch, and Dodge listened to little of it. He hoped Rock would go to bed and give him a chance to talk to Uncle Bill. But this appeared unlikely, so presently Dodge went to the far end of the porch and climbed the ladder to his corner of the loft. He shared that part of it with saddles, rolls of canvas, sacks of grain, and other articles. Before undressing, he sat a while on his bed, which was one of the luxuries in this new life. The wind moaned in the pines and branches rustled on the roof over his head. The stream music, too, was sad. Low voices of the brothers came to his ears. Bill, despite his doubts, was talking with earnest persuasion. Mercer believed he might just as well talk to the cliffs. Finally, when stretched out on his bed, he thought of something. He gave the upright log near his head a gentle rap. Then he placed his ear against it. Almost instantly a soft answer came up. Then he rapped twice, to be signaled as readily. Pausing then, with his charged emotions in abeyance, he tapped three times. No answer! But as he lay there in the pitchy blackness something mystical in the night something out of the tragedy of this household, persuaded him that not forever would his love signal be received in silence.

Long before midnight Dodge, sleepless and pondering, connected the barking of the pups with faint sounds of activity out in the fields. He sat up. The Lilley cabin seemed wrapped in slumber. But it was not. Soft footfalls padded across the porch below. One of the boys pulled on his boots and made off into the darkness.

Dodge got into his clothes, except his boots, which he carried, and noiselessly he descended the ladder and went out into the yard. There was something afoot, perhaps only a prank of the boys, but he decided to see. Pulling on his boots, he felt his way through the trees out into the open. How bright the stars! The dark rim stood up grandly. And the canyon country below showed as dim and opaque as it was mysterious by day. He heard threshing sounds down in the sorghum field.

He approached the field from the east end of the clearing, where the forest afforded cover. By this time his eyes had grown accustomed to the darkness. He made out the first shocks of sorghum, then a number of horses. Low voices and an unguarded laugh guided him. Presently from behind a shock he saw dark forms of men. They were carrying armloads of sorghum. Dodge deliberated. It appeared to be an irregular proceeding. It justified his interference. He drew closer, under cover of one shock after another, then boldly strode out to confront them.

"Thet you, Steve? You—loafer! About time you got here!" called a voice with a ring in it.

"No, it's not Steve," retorted Mercer sharply. "What the devil are you fellows doing this time of night? Stealing Lilley's sorghum?"

"Who'n hell blazes air you?" demanded the tall fellow with the ringing voice. He was young, leonine of build, violent.

Dodge shoved his gun into the man's hard stomach until he doubled up like a jackknife.

"Get out of this, you measly nighthawks!" ordered Mercer.

One of the dark figures broke into a run. His boots thudded away in the direction of the Lilley cabin, and it was Mercer's guess that he belonged there.

The tall fellow stumbled over a bundle of sorghum and fell flat. Dodge gave him a resounding kick.

"You sorghum rustlers! Hop your horses pronto or I'll loose this gun on you."

Two of them were active and silent. The big one pulled himself up hissing like a snake.

"All right, we'll go, but by Gawd, whoever you are, you'll hear of this," he burst out stridently.

"Shut up, Hathaway!" flashed Dodge, sure of his man. "I'm acting on my own judgment. This deal looks queer to me. I'd just as lief shoot you as not."

"Queer or not, mister, this here sorghum is *mine* an' this land is *mine*," declared the other harshly.

"I don't know that. Come around in the daylight and prove it," concluded Dodge.

Rapidly they rode off in the darkness, and presently Dodge heard the loud-mouthed one cursing and raving to his comrades.

Dodge hurried back to try to locate the one that had run off, or possibly Steve Lilley, who had certainly been expected. But he neither saw nor heard either of them, and finally arrived at the cabin, bayed by the hounds. They knew him now, however, and soon quieted down. Dodge climbed to his bed and lay down, this time without undressing. If there had been anything to regret in going out to the fields he could not yet discern it. Indeed he welcomed what had happened. He had too long been accustomed to the violence of the frontier to be undecided. He would await developments, however, before speaking of this night's adventure.

Next morning members of the Lilley household appeared one by one, long after Dodge had arisen to walk and sit about, waiting for breakfast.

He did not avail himself of an opportunity to speak with Nan, whose anxious gaze he felt. It was Steve that Dodge wished to corner; and after this surly brother had been waited upon by Nan, to slouch off the porch, Dodge followed him down toward the barn.

"Hey, Steve, hold on," he called. If anything, the young man strode faster. Whereupon Dodge ran to catch up with him, to detain him with no light hand. "I reckon we'd better have a friendly little powwow."

"Wal, I don't reckon," replied Steve sullenly. He was a handsome lad of nineteen, the only one of the brothers who resembled Nan. And Dodge had observed two important things in Steve's relation to the difficult situation there: Nan loved him; and to Dodge there were unmistakable signs that Steve had departed from the straight and narrow path. At any cost Dodge must propitiate this lad, make a friend of him, and thereafter influence him for good.

"Then you'll listen without reckoning," replied Dodge, and with a powerful arm he dragged Steve off the trail into the pine brush and spun him around like a top. "Are you looking for trouble?"

"Cain't stay thet," returned Steve resentfully. The clean brown tan had paled.

"Very well, then listen," went on Dodge deliberately. "I'm not a liar, and you'll do better to see in me a friend. If you won't see me as yours, then you've got to see me as Nan's. Is that clear?"

"I can hear," returned young Lilley stubbornly.

"There's hell to pay in this family, and I'm on the track of it. I've a hunch it's this hellish rotgut you call white mule. You're drinking it, Steve. Some way or other you're mixed up in the distilling of it. Last night proved that. Well, you're too young and fine a lad to ruin your health and life with such stuff. Break Nan's heart! I'm going to stop you one way or another. Now does that straight talk get into you?"

Steve did not admit it by word of mouth, but his flopping down on a log in shame and dismay was more eloquent than speech.

"What does Nan know?" he queried huskily. "Damn her! She's told you somethin'."

"No, Steve. Only that there was trouble in your family. I've had to find out what I could and guess the rest."

"Who'n hell air you to come meddlin' in our business?" burst out Steve, in an amazed anger.

"Easy. I'm a friend in need. Nan's and yours. And of all you Lilleys. Never mind how it happened. Just believe me. Then we can get somewhere. Steve, think clear if you can. This was bad business before I came. It's worse now—*because I'll end it*. Do you savvy? You went out last night to help pack the sorghum. One of your brothers went, too. I'm not asking you to give him or anyone away."

"But what you want then?" interrupted Steve desperately.

"Only for you to listen to sense. Will you do that?"

"Go on," returned Steve, in muffled tones.

"This white mule is killing your dad. He thinks he's got cancer. But it's nothing else than your kicking sorghum juice. If I don't miss my guess he'll die before long. He's all gone inside. That's going to be a blow to you—to Nan—to all of you."

"Aw, it ain't so. Dad ain't thet sick," cried Steve hoarsely.

"Yes, it is so. Uncle Bill knows it. We've all known it too late for him."

"Dodge, I—I hate the damn stuff," declared the boy passionately.

"Then why do you drink it, Steve?" queried Dodge, his hand going to Steve's shoulder.

[56]

"Aw, they all drink except Hathaway, an' I fell in with them."

"Couldn't you quit it?"

"I reckon if I could stay away from Hathaway," rejoined Steve miserably. "But you see, Dodge, I've no other way to earn money. Dad takes every dollar we all earn here—if he knows aboot it. We're only a passel of slaves. An' I've got a—a sweetheart in Ryeson. She's run after by fellars who can buy her pretty things. An' I've had to hump myself. I went in debt at Timms'. If I could only get a job that'd pay me a little I'd tell Buck Hathaway to go plumb to hell with his white mule!"

"Now you're talking!" exclaimed Dodge ringingly. "Say, I'm glad I ran after you. Steve, this is going to be easy."

"Wal, you talk big."

"I'm taking you at your word. Is your word of honor good?"

"No Lilley ever breaks his word," replied Steve stoutly.

For many a month prior to this western flight Dodge had added every dollar possible to his savings. And now that money would serve him in good stead.

"Steve, while my money lasts it's yours as much as mine. Here. Pay your debts. Let's work to build up this run-down ranch. I'm a cattleman. I can see this range grazing ten thousand head. Stand up and shake on the deal."

Steve leaped up, a bewildered and transformed lad. Like magic the ugly traces vanished from his reddening face, and his big eyes glowed with something of the wonder of Nan's.

"Dodge, I cain't—I oughtn't take this money. But I—"

"Why not? I've plenty more. We're pards now."

"By Gawd, Nan was right," he ejaculated, and subjected Dodge's hand to a squeeze which almost crushed the bones of that precious member.

"I hope so. But what did she say?"

"Never mind. It was shore too much fer me to swaller. Bless thet gurl's heart! Dodge, I'm glad you come. An' I'll stand by you till hell freezes over."

Then he rushed away, leaving Dodge in a glow of gladness. "So far so good! Nan, what're you going to say to that?" he soliloquized, and sat down to add some more links to the chain he was forging. Buck Hathaway was the ringleader in whatever kind of shady business the Lilleys had become involved. How many greedy, grasping men Dodge had run across in his range riding! What infinite variety of means by which gullible people were ensnared! Yet the genius in every case was the same—some villain or thief or crafty seeker grasping to himself woman, stock, land, water, money.

Dodge almost convinced himself that his first conjecture had been wrong. The Lilleys scarcely had a moonshine still of their own. No doubt the Hathaways operated one, perhaps with the connivance of some of the Lilley boys, or at least their assistance. The night raid on the sorghum seemed to intimate something secret in connection with the distillation of the liquor. Certainly the making of moonshine whisky was criminal in any state or territory. Revenue officers, however, were hardly to be imagined as knowing of this remote Arizona fastness. It struck Dodge then, rather singularly, that the drinking of white mule was in no wise the disgraceful thing that seemed to hold for its manufacture.

After a while his thoughts worked around to consideration of a meeting with Buck Hathaway, a circumstance very likely to occur this summer day. In whatever light he regarded it there was little of the cold questioning, the dark and fateful doubt, that had been sure to confront Dodge Mercer back on the wild frontier of the Panhandle, when he had been driven to the corner familiar to all true gunmen. A backwoodsman could have but little of the knowledge, experience, and skill that were necessary to enable riders like Dodge to survive. If the moonshiner packed a gun and attempted to draw it, then the ugly necessity would be quickly passed, and Dodge could devote himself to the less formidable of the Lilley troubles.

CHAPTER 5

Riders passing up the trail toward the cabin disrupted Dodge's sober train of thought. The Lilleys were certainly going to have company. He peeped out through the pine foliage, to obtain close view of six or eight mounted horses, two of whose riders were feminine. It was a merry party. But it did not include the leonine figure that Dodge felt grimly sure he would recognize. Not desiring to follow immediately, he spent another half-hour in reflection, and then made his way back to the cabin.

The big porch presented a colorful contrast to its usual drab, homely appearance. Bright blankets hung over the rail; the hounds were all present, excited and whining, knowing well this would be an occasion for them; the boys shone spick-and-span in their Sunday suits and gaudy scarfs; the women visitors resembled gay birds of brilliant plumage. And the Lilley girls wore white. When Dodge picked Nan out he experienced a shock of rapture.

Steve came down the steps to meet him, a quick-stepping, clean-garbed Steve from whose features had vanished the somber brooding, the significant flush of heat, the furtive, downcast glance.

"Dodge, I told Nan," he whispered. "Thet aboot Dad— an' you an' me. Now you're in fer it! Nan'll eat you alive."

"Gosh! Did you tell her about Hathaway—about where that white mule comes from?"

"No. She was so sick aboot Dad an' so glad aboot me thet she near busted. I hadn't the heart to tell more. But thet'll hev to be told. An' then spittin' cougars won't be nothin' to Nan. There'll shore be hell around this ranch."

They mounted the steps together, and Steve's arm was linked in Dodge's as he led him to a pretty little girl like nothing so much as a wild rose.

"Tess, this heah is my new pard, Dodge Mercer, from Kansas. Dodge, meet my gurl, Tess Williams."

"Mister Dodge, yore ears must be burnin' from all I hear said aboot you," replied the girl, in a happy mingling of shy and arch delight.

"Well, so you're Tess?" replied Mercer, squeezing her extended hand. "The pleasure's all mine, little lady."

At that juncture a small brown hand slipped under Dodge's arm on the right side, and its pressure, as well as sight of its owner, vibrated through all his being.

"Dodge, aren't they just the nicest couple—my brother and Tess?" asked Nan.

"Nice! Why, I'd call them just wonderful," declared Dodge.

"I reckon you've both kissed the blarney stone," said Tess.

"Yes, an' they'll be kissin' somethin' else before long," added Steve devilishly.

Nan whirled Dodge around, the color high in her cheeks. "Dodge, you must meet the other folks," she said, and then whispered wildly: "You're my good angel! Oh, Steve is his old self today! What have you done?"

"Nan, I reckon I scared him first, then talked sense," replied Dodge. "Introduce me around to your company. Steve's girl, Tess, near cut you out, Nan."

"So I saw, Mister Mercer. It's better that I kept you from takin' *all* my breath. Here's Tess's sister and she's even prettier."

Soon Dodge found himself very pleasantly engaged, so much so that he almost forgot to keep a sharp lookout for Hathaway. Having detected a slightly jealous note in Nan's voice, Dodge devoted himself to Tess's sister. He soon found, however, that she was too frank and nice a girl to be treated insincerely even for one moment. He was careful, however, to make it appear that he had forgotten Nan's existence.

Dodge knew he was the first to see three riders emerge from the forest below and ride out of sight toward the corrals. The only other person who made this observation was Nan, and she telegraphed Dodge a warning look. One of these incoming riders was Buck Hathaway. Presently the three came in sight down the wide pine-shaded lane. The taller was in the lead, and walked rather violently.

"Heah comes Buck now," spoke up one of the young men.

That riveted the attention of all on the approaching trio. Uncle Bill spoke in an undertone to his brother Rock.

"Aw, no! Not on a Sunday—comin' heah!" protested the chief.

"Shore looks like it," replied Bill.

"Wal, if Buck's lookin' for trouble he'll git—"

Lilley was interrupted by his son Steve, who had been standing at the porch rail watching Hathaway approach.

"Paw, it's Buck an' he shore looks ugly," said Steve. And then he swerved his glance to Dodge. His eyes were bright and flashing. Aside from the absence of warning, they resembled Nan's so closely as to fix Dodge's swift thoughts. This was the moment. No time like the present! In a clash between enemies, as well as rivals, the first blow, like the first shot, was sure to be telling. It was quite natural then that Dodge, before acting upon his sudden inspiration, should take a searching look at his adversary.

Buck Hathaway slowed his stride as he neared the porch. He was tall and had bulky shoulders. His big bare head held a mop of thick yellow hair that appeared to stand up like a mane. This had given him the leonine look. He was undeniably handsome with a fierce godlike cast of features. Halting at the bottom of the steps, he glanced up an instant and then half-turned to address his comrades close behind. His profile was singularly sharp, and it was at this angle that he appeared most prepossessing. Then he faced back again and took a step up. His eyes were large, flaring, gray or light blue, and brutal in expression. His nose was long and straight, remarkable for its distended nostrils. He had large curved lips, just now opening to a slight sneer. Altogether, his face showed a heat that came only partially from physical activity, mostly from rage.

Dodge took in all these details after he had ascertained that Hathaway carried a gun on his hip—a circumstance that had instantly clarified the rather difficult situation.

When Hathaway had mounted to within a couple of steps to the porch level, Dodge sprang erect in pretended great excitement. But the fact that his leap placed him in the middle of the porch with the open space between the two cabins directly behind him would have been illuminating to these backwoods folk if Uncle Bill had explained the reason.

Dodge pointed an accusing finger at Hathaway and called out piercingly: "Lilley, that's the fellow I drove out of your field last night. He was stealing your sorghum."

The blank silence that ensued proved to Dodge that he had caused even more consternation than he had hoped for.

Hathaway's face turned a livid scarlet, but Dodge surmised that the fellow's emotion was not shame.

"Rock," he burst out, "you send this fellar out of here, or, by Gawd, I'll drive him!"

Dodge took a step forward. "Look here, Hathaway, I've never been broke to driving." Dodge's voice, his look, the manner in which he stood meant little if anything to this backwoods Arizonian.

"You'll be broke to more'n thet before this day's over," returned Hathaway stridently.

"Haw! Haw!" Uncle Bill edged into the situation with

short, cold laughter. Perhaps it surprised Dodge less than anyone else present.

"Who're you laughin' at?" demanded Hathaway hotly.

"Buck, you shore strike me funny," retorted the Texan.

"Ahuh. So I had a hunch before. Wal, you might be takin' yoreself off with this Kansas cowhand."

Rock Lilley at last came out of his stupefaction and when he stamped to his feet his chair went with a crash.

"Buck Hathaway, hev you come rarin' in heah on a Sunday?" he roared.

"Sunday's nuthin' to me, Rock. I ain't waitin' another mawnin'."

"Man, you're crazy!"

"Hell! I ain't crazy, an' I wouldn't care a damn if I was."

"What's it all aboot?" interposed Uncle Bill, who certainly understood Dodge's needs of the moment. It thrilled Dodge to see that Nan, white-faced and wide of eye, had gravitated to the Texan's side.

"I'm sorry if I've—but I can't understand how *I* can be in the wrong," hurriedly replied Dodge. "My training has been to be responsible for what's left in my charge. Lilley, last night I heard something down in the sorghum field. I slipped on my clothes and boots and ran down there. I ran plumb into this fellow Hathaway with three others stealing your sorghum. They had your pack horses. I threw my gun on them and drove them away, same as I would any other kind of rustlers."

"Stealin' Rock Lilley's sorghum!" exclaimed Hathaway

derisively. "Thet's a good one. I'll laugh myself. Haw! Haw! Haw!"

"You can't bluff me," retorted Dodge, working up a pretended anger. "You were stealing that sorghum and I can prove it."

"Shore you was stealin' it," added Uncle Bill. "I saw yore tracks this mawnin'. An' I've missed shocks of sorghum oot of thet field every mawnin' since we've been cuttin'."

"Buck, get oot of heah, will you? This ain't no day to start a mess before my folks and company."

Lilley was plainly perturbed, but he did not react to this situation as Dodge had expected him to.

"Rock, your word is law among your people. But you cain't stall me off with bluffs about company or Sunday. I'm here, an' if you know what's good fer you, this Kansas cowhand will get a hunch to make himself scarce. An' I'm hintin' mebbe Uncle Bill has had quite a long visit."

"Rock, you let this Hathaway bully talk like this in your own house?" demanded Uncle Bill, in wrathful outrage. "It ain't decent. I just cain't figger you."

"Hold on, will you?" roared Lilley thickly. "I cain't help Hathaway's rarin' in heah. But I shore wouldn't stand fer his orderin' my company or my help aboot."

Dodge believed that this was the crucial moment to force the issue.

"Lilley, I'm to blame for this mess. I'm sorry. But it's gone too far now. What I want to know is this. Wasn't this fellow Hathaway and his men *stealing* your sorghum?"

"Thet's what we want to know," added Uncle Bill, with fire in his eye.

Lilley choked and utterance died in his throat. He was a cornered if not a beaten man.

Then Steve leaped up from the bench beside the rail. "Dad, this is shore a dirty mix for Dodge. He's perfectly right in thinkin' Hathaway stole the sorghum. I was out there helpin' pack it. So was Ben, if he's got guts enough to tell you. Buck had a hold on us both. I needed money bad. An' he paid me fer packin' an' workin'. Thet's how I got to drinkin' his damned white mule. But I've quit him, Dad, I've quit, an' you kin thank Dodge for it."

Lilley sagged back to right his chair and sink into it, his face ashen, his jaw wobbling.

"Steve Lilley, you've double-crossed me," declared Hathaway fiercely. "You'll pay for that, Skunk! Showin' off before your girl an' this Kansas cowhand!"

"I don't know what it is, Buck, but I've been thankin' God I had the nerve. Now you lay off me, or you'll git another jar."

Dodge pushed Steve back out of line. "Thanks, boy, but that's about all for you. This is my mix and it's a dirty one. Rock, I quit my job. I'm no guest in your house. Mister Hathaway has seen fit to insult me. That's *my* affair."

Hathaway might have been devoid of fear, in any event, but his rage was such that it gave the impression that it would betray his mastery of the situation.

Uncle Bill was yet to be reckoned with.

"Hathaway, I don't quite savvy Steve's talk. I'm askin'

you straight. Didn't Dodge ketch you packin' our sorghum?"

"An' who's Dodge?"

"This fellar you're so pleased to call a Kansas cowhand. He's Dodge Mercer. Does thet mean anythin' to you?"

"Nuthin'. An' I don't feel partickler honored," sneered Hathaway. "But if it's any of *your* mix, yes, he did ketch us packin' sorghum."

"All right. Do you reckon you was stealin' it?"

"Hell, no! Thet sorghum is mine. An' this land heah, this cabin heah, air mine."

"Ahuh. An' how air they?"

"I've a lien on this ranch."

"Ahuh. I'm beginnin' to see. An' how come?"

"Yore brother owes me twice as much money as this land an' stock air worth."

"Hev you any proof of thet?"

"Shore. Rock's word."

Uncle Bill turned to his brother. "Rock, is it so?"

"Yes. My—word—an' it's—good," replied Lilley hoarsely.

The Texan manifestly considered his part in the sordid revelation had been played out, and his slight gesture to Dodge seemed conclusive and significant. Then he stepped back, leaving the middle of the porch occupied by Dodge. Those spectators who had been lined along the rail at first had gradually edged back on each side. Hathaway had remained all this while standing on the first and second steps, but now he strode up on the porch, his opaque eyes, hot and hateful, fastened upon Dodge.

[68]

At this juncture Nan bounded out to confront Hathaway.

"So it was you?" she flashed, in shrill scorn. She seemed the embodiment of fury. Dodge did not take his gaze off his adversary, yet he appeared to see Nan's white face and blazing eyes.

"Yeah, it was me," returned Hathaway, not in the least perturbed by Nan's flashing affront. He had maintained from the first a harsh, consistent, evil wrath, which he seemingly held righteous.

"Buck Hathaway, it's you who brought shame an' ruin upon my dad—all of us," she cried huskily. "I always felt you were no good. An' now I hate you. My dad gave his word thet I marry you. But I break it. Here and now! I wouldn't marry you to save us all from starvin' to death."

"Nan Lilley, you shut up!" he replied, stung to the quick. "Your dad's word is law. An' you're not your own boss."

"Did you hear me? I hate you!"

"Aw, you're all riled up by this mess. It ain't what you think. I've been drove nigh mad, Nan."

There was a suggestion of dignity and appeal in his words, if not in his stern, unyielding front.

"You'll be drove worse if you don't clear out. I'm through with you. Dad can't change me. You can't either. If I had guessed it was *you* . . . My dad—my brother Steve—and Ben! Oh, get out of here, Buck Hathaway!"

His thick hide seemed to have been penetrated, and he became an image of malignant force. Wheeling to Lilley, he demanded: "Rock, you hear this dutiful girl of yours! This Nan Lilley! Does what she says go with you?"

"Buck, I haven't any say over her feelin's," replied Lilley brokenly. "But if you still want her—after thet—wal, my word is good."

"Thar, Nan, you hear?" declared Hathaway stridently, his shaking hand outheld. "All this row for nuthin'!"

"I'll die first! *You lousy moonshiner!*" flamed Nan, her words like coals of fire flung in his face.

He recoiled. That epithet, unspoken before, had power to flay.

"So thet's more I've got to thank your Kansas cowhand for?" he choked out, his eyes narrowed to fiery slits, his face gray and corded.

But he did not intimidate her. Nan, like Steve, showed the blood of the Lilleys. There seemed to be a subtle intimation in Hathaway's query.

"I reckon you have, Mister Hathaway," she replied, as if driven to a truth she would rather have concealed. Uncle Bill reached out a long arm and drew her aside to leave Hathaway alone with Dodge.

"You cow-rastlin' meddler!" yelled Hathaway, and swung his right arm in a long side sweep.

Dodge could certainly have dodged that slap. But he took it, square on cheek and chin, and it staggered him.

"Look out, everybody!" interposed Uncle Bill, spreading wide his arms to force Nan, Steve, and Tess, and several others farther back. "By Gawd, the yappin' fool has brought it on his own haid!"

Dodge recovered his equilibrium, and with his left

hand felt of the smarting blow to his face. He no longer feigned anger that he did not truly feel. Contempt for this lout merely increased, and with it that cold, strange certainty of what he intended to deal. But since Nan's brave and startling declaration, Dodge did not want to kill Hathaway before her very eyes if he could help it. He parried for time.

"So you hit me, Hathaway?" he queried, slow and cool.

"Wal, if you didn't feel thet one, I'll try again," sneered the backwoodsman, now sure of himself, and nursing his intent.

"Take a look at that," retorted Dodge suddenly, as he thrust out his right hand. It was indeed a strong, brown, supple, strangely suggestive and beautiful member. "Buck, I haven't hit a man with that hand for ten years. Never dug fence-post holes or such like jobs cowhands hate. Never wore a glove on it! Does that mean anything to you, Hathaway?"

"Aw, hell! It shore don't—no more than your soft-soap gab," replied Hathaway, but he was lying, for that hand or something about it or in Dodge's vague words had plainly fascinated him.

"I reckoned you wouldn't, so there's no sense in telling you why I can't return the compliment with it," drawled Dodge. "But I can use this one."

Suddenly, with swiftness amazing after his slow manner and drawling speech, he shot out his left fist to strike Hathaway a hard blow square on nose and mouth. Hathaway fell his full length, with sodden heaviness, and his head and shoulder went over the edge of the porch. He caught himself, however, with his right hand or elbow on the first step. His face was that of a surprised and furious beast. Blood began to pour from his nose down over his mouth and chin. Something in that face, in the glaring eyes, or the violence just exerted, unleashed the savage in Dodge. In another moment, if he did not render Hathaway helpless, he would have to follow up that blow with a shot. Quick as a cat he leaped, and swinging his leg he kicked Hathaway off the porch. Hathaway flopped down the steps to thud soddenly upon the ground.

Dodge took two steps down, with his gun out and half leveled. Hathaway lay face up, his legs still on the lower steps. His face was a bloody blotch, and he appeared badly stunned, but he was not unconscious.

"Drag him away, you fellows," ordered Dodge sharply. "Rustle—or I'll kill him!"

The two comrades laid quick hold on Hathaway and began to lift and draw him down the path. They got him to his feet, but he could not stand without their support. He appeared to be hissing and moaning. They gazed back with scared faces.

"Tell him if he ever meets me again to pull a gun," called Dodge after them, and he waited until they were out of sight before he faced the porch again. Slowly he ascended the steps, sheathing his gun. Rock Lilley rose to meet him, and Dodge saw what this man had been before destroying liquor had devastated his physical and moral fiber.

"Lilley, I don't see how I could have done anything else," said Dodge apologetically. "I'm sorry to upset you—

spoil your Sunday—and get Nan in more trouble. But the damned thing just happened. I'll say, though, but for Nan, I'd have killed him."

"Wal, why in hell didn't you? I reckon Nan could hev stood it," returned the backwoodsman grimly. "You ride in here, mess up things generally, an' then never finish the job."

"But it was all accident, Lilley. How could I know?"

"Hell, man, do you reckon I've no sense at all?" retorted Lilley gruffly. "Mebbe thet about your goin' to the sorghum field was accident. Mebbe. But the rest was a slick job. You an' Nan an' Uncle Bill here put it up on me. Steve, too. But don't mistake me, Mercer. I'm partickler glad fer Steve. I knowed somethin' was wrong with thet boy. Buck was shore mean. An' he drives a hard bargain. But so long as I live my word is good. Thet's all."

Nan stepped forward unsteadily, shaken and distraught.

"Dad, please don't send Dodge away."

"Wal, lass, who said anythin' about thet? He jest quit. I reckon, mebbe, you kin git him to change his mind. Haw! Haw!"

Whereupon Lilley, sagging a little, as if under a weight, went into the cabin. His wife followed.

"Oh, Dodge, he accused us," whispered Nan tearfully. "But that wasn't fair. It just came about. Oh, only for Dad now I'd be happy."

"It's tough on him, Nan, but better all the way round."

"No, no. Poor old Dad! He'll never lift his head again."

"Wal, Nan," spoke up Uncle Bill, "thet'd be better than the way it was goin'."

She gazed up at Dodge with tear-wet, unashamed, and worshipful eyes. "Dodge, you have freed us." Then she fled.

Uncle Bill drew Dodge away to the far corner of the porch.

"Not so bad fer a Kansas cowhand," he chuckled. "But thet Hathaway never woke up. Shore, Dodge, I seen your side of it. Fer you to draw on him would hev been murder pure an' simple. But I reckon you ought to hev done it. Because when you do meet you'll hev to kill him. An' he'll waylay you along the trails."

"Thanks, Uncle Bill. I'll not take any chances. It was rough on old Rock. I meant to force things, but— Well, I'd have done it anyhow."

"Shore. You done jest what I figgered 'cept you didn't kill him when you had the excuse. Wal, wal! It's out now an' nuthin' but good shall come of it. Say, did you see Nan when she called Hathaway a lousy moonshiner?"

"No, not straight. I had to keep my eyes on him. But Nan's voice was enough for me. And his face! Wow!"

"My Gawd, you should hev seen her. Nan's a Lilley, all right."

"Bill, I reckon I'll sneak off in the woods for a little while."

The Sunday dinner was not a success. Rock Lilley did not come out, nor did Ben show himself again. Steve appeared to be the only one not subdued and silent. Once or twice, when Dodge caught Nan watching him from inside the cabin, he felt both remorse and rapture. In the shadow, her eyes expressed the havoc he had brought to her. But at last, when finally she sat at the table, she appeared pale but composed and appeared not to notice him.

Soon after dinner the visitors rode away. Dodge spent the afternoon in the woods and did not return until he had watched the sun set. Uncle Bill and Rock smoked their pipes as usual on the porch, but the brown jug was conspicuous by its absence. The scared children gradually recovered, still only little Rock ventured near Dodge. Soon they were put to bed. Dodge sat on the porch steps hoping Nan would come out, but he hoped in vain.

He was left alone, a prey to gloomy thoughts, despite all the hopeful aspects of the case. Then he climbed to his loft and went to bed. Scarcely had his head touched the pillow when a faint rap came up the log. He started, placed his ear to the pine upright, and gently tapped it once. That was his answer, to what he feared he had only imagined. Two taps came up. This was no lying trick of his hope. Nan had called him. With his heart going to his throat he answered her, then waited with abated breath. There seemed a long interval, fraught with dying eagerness, deadening thrill. Then came a rap—another, very faint, and finally a third, sharp, quick, electrifying, as if all weakness had succumbed to a wild, sweet surrender. Dodge answered in a transport.

CHAPTER 6

One dark morning Dodge slipped away from the Lilleys' ostensibly to hunt for some of the half-wild cattle that roamed the woods freely and had not been rounded up or cared for in a long time. More important, he wanted to see if he could locate Hathaway's still, and possibly destroy the source of the white mule. He had informed Uncle Bill about his intention and that worthy had just wagged his grizzled head, offering no opinion.

As he rode deeper into the forest, the first flush of dawn changed the steely sky to rose over the dark fringed rim of the great wall of canyoned rock. The rose turned to gold, and burst gloriously into the rising of the sun.

Soon he headed off the well-defined Rock Rim trail into the thickets of scrub oak and jack pine, manzanita and mescal, and began to climb a seldom-used trail on which he found old horse tracks. It led over the slope to the mesa, into the cedars and junipers and piñons, and at last into the somber forest again.

Here it was like twilight, cool, still, and lonely. The peace of the wilderness tried to pierce Dodge's brooding thoughts of the problem of Hathaway and his white mule, but it did not succeed. Even thought of Nan failed to dispel his gloom. Hours passed swiftly as Dodge climbed high and traversed miles, in a multitude of detours and zigzags, more than a thousand feet above the basin below. The slopes grew exceedingly wild and rough. The pines gave way again to smaller growth. In many places he dismounted to climb on foot. How dry the brush and soil were. The tufts of grass were sere and brown; the dead manzanita broke like icicles.

At length he arrived at the base of the Rock Rim wall itself. It still towered above him, seemingly to the sky. Another faint trail bisected the one he was following and ran along the irregular stone cliff. Here he found much fresher hoof tracks, perhaps a day old, he decided.

Dodge rode on to a corner of the wall. The trail plunged down again. A mighty amphitheater opened in the Rim. It was miles across and extended far back. All around the capes and escarpments loomed out over the colorful abyss. Yellow crags leaned with their great slabs of rock tottering out over the void. Here and there gleamed cliffs of dull pink, with black eyelike caves. Far down in the middle of this gulf meandered a dark canyon.

Dodge was certain that Hathaway would not have founded his base of operations on top of the Rock Rim because of the heavy winter snows. But somewhere in this maze of wilderness he faced would be a likely hiding place, warm in winter and most difficult of location. For a long time he looked and watched. He saw nothing that moved, no sign of any smoke. A distant rumble of thunder behind him caused him to turn around.

The sun was sinking, and through great masses of black cloud it shed a gleam of angry red. From the southwest a lowering multitude of pale little clouds came scudding toward the Rim. They were the heralds of a storm. But as yet, except for the moan of the wind in the cliff, there was no sound. The basin lay deep in blue and purple shadow. The gray tones near at hand, the smoky sulphurous red of the sunset, the utter solitude, the vast cliff-toothed gap in the Rim, the calling, forbidding shadow of the gorge, the all-pervading spirit of nature's inevitable and ruthless change from lull to storm—all these permeated Dodge's being, and possessed him utterly. He turned back to the trail and gazed down with narrowed eyes. What an inaccessible place! It could hide a hundred men, a dozen stills. There came a sudden rush of wind, wailing in the niches of the cliffs overhead, presaging the nearness of the storm.

This time Dodge saw a log cabin somewhat below and to his right. Its door evidently faced away from him to the east. This would afford some protection for the night, and he was certain it would be deserted. Hathaway would not tarry long where he could be seen from far off and easily found.

A few hundred yards down the trail before it disappeared from sight Dodge saw an outcropping of ledge, level enough to cross and not leave any tracks. He led Baldy down, and soon was slipping and sliding into a narrow ravine, rock filled and heavily covered with pine needles. It was treacherous going. Several times Baldy went down on his haunches and Dodge had to run to keep ahead of the horse.

Sudden tension on the bridle reins brought Dodge up short. Baldy had stepped into a hole, his right foreleg down between rocks. He stood still, trembling. One abrupt move would break that leg.

"Whoa, boy, easy—easy," Dodge called softly as he came up beside the horse.

Dodge patted Baldy's neck and put his shoulder against him. Slowly, slowly Baldy pulled his leg up and out. Dodge sighed in relief.

"I should have known better. Fine backwoodsman I am," he said in disgust.

From there on to the mouth of the draw they stayed on the edge against the steep slope. Soon they came out onto a fairly level bench at the end of which Dodge saw the cabin under a dark spear-pointed fir tree. Off to one side was a small clump of spruce where he left Baldy. He would reconnoiter first, make sure the place was deserted.

Dodge made a complete circle some distance away. There were no discernible tracks leading to or from the old log structure. He returned to get Baldy and led him close to the door, dropping the reins. Unconcerned, Baldy lowered his head to tear off a mouthful of yellow grass.

The open door stared wide and unblinking. It was dark inside and smelled dry and musty. No one had been here for a long time. Dodge heard the rustling of mice, the whining of bats from the entrance. He sank to a seat on the broken doorsill. His sombrero fell off unheeded as raindrops fell on his face and began to patter on the old shake roof. Dodge saw with surprise that there were no holes in the roof, although in places the chinks had fallen out from between the logs. Who had built this place, when, and why?

Presently Dodge busied himself with necessary tasks. He located a small spring not far away where he slipped the bridle and let Baldy drink. Then he lay down to partake himself of the clear, cold water. He unsaddled, fed Baldy half of the grain he had brought along, and turned him loose. Dodge had acquired the horse as a colt and made a pet of him. He had never strayed.

The rain had steadily increased in volume and Dodge was glad to find shelter inside the old cabin. He opened the small pack and ate some of the meat and biscuits he had remembered to bring along. It was getting cooler, but Dodge decided against building a fire. Too risky. He sat just inside the doorway looking out into the twilight. Baldy grazed a few steps away. Dodge fought against the depression and loneliness that seized him. And finally his imagination overcame it and he saw a fire in a fireplace, glaring coals in which there seemed to appear a sweet face with dark blue haunting eyes, red lips, a sweet and sad smile. Above the patter of the rain and the mourning of the wind he heard again one, two, and a third light tap on the cabin wall.

It was dark now and Dodge discovered he was tired. He lay down, put his head on the saddle, and pulled the blanket over him. In no time he drifted into slumber.

When Dodge awakened the rain had stopped. The

forest smell was fresh and clean. Something seemed to be bothering him and he decided it was the fact that he had as yet made no definite plan of action in attempting to seek out Hathaway's still. Then, as he was attending to the few morning necessities such as food and water for Baldy and himself, he formulated one.

He climbed back to the faint trail farther up and over a less perilous route than the previous evening's descent and followed the tracks of two shod horses—careful to stop and look and listen at each turning. Dodge was sure that sooner or later he would intercept yet another trail, or more than one. It was certain there was more than one way in and out of this huge, lonely hole in the Rim.

When the sun finally rose above the east wall of the canyon it began to get hot. Soon, however, the trail descended into ever-thickening forest and Dodge heard below him the sound of a brook rushing over rocks. This must be the headwaters of the creek that ran near the Lilley ranch.

Hour after hour Dodge rode along the narrow defile, around boulders that grew increasingly large. He flushed a bunch of wild turkeys at which he did not dare shoot. Now and then through a hole in the dense woods he could see the Rim to the east or west. The walls seemed to be getting closer together and the mouths of side canyons were narrower. Once he heard the sound of rolling stones across the creek and had a momentary glimpse of a black bear crossing a slide. Suddenly he came to another trail bisecting the one he was following. On it, coming up from the bottom of the gorge and leading to the west, were fresh horse tracks. The older tracks turned to the east on this trail, and Dodge caught a whiff of wood smoke although he could see none. In fact, he could not see more than fifty yards in any direction. He decided to backtrack to the east on foot, and he led Baldy some distance back along the way he had come and tied him behind a house-sized, moss-covered rock. He removed his chaps and hung them over the saddle horn, reached for his rifle, then thought better of taking it. There was not enough open ground to make it of much use if he ran into anyone. His Colt would be enough.

Back at the intercepting trails he took off toward the sound of the running water. Soon he was zigzagging down into the very bottom of the canyon. There came the sound of a waterfall from downstream. Dodge thought he heard the sliding of rocks somewhere behind him, but he could not be sure. Finally he reached the stream. Here it flowed quietly through a long, shallow, gravelly pool and disappeared below around a corner of cliff from whence came the noise of the fall. He could see the horse tracks leading down the opposite bank, emerging near the spot where he stood. The water was clear and cold. About fifty feet below there were rocks protruding above the surface. He skirted along the bank and started across.

Suddenly he felt the terrific impact of a bullet as a heavy rifle shot rang out from the slope above and behind him. He fell into the creek and lay face downward, not moving. A little way downstream there was cover. If his assailant would only believe the ambush had succeeded in killing him outright and not shoot again! Dodge lay still, and drifted with the current. When he could no longer hold his breath he risked turning his head to gulp for air. He saw that he was opposite another huge boulder on the shore. There was no sound from the slope, no sound of any kind except the murmuring stream and, below, the waterfall.

Dodge cursed himself for a fool. He had been too sure. As quietly as possible he crawled out of the water, behind the big rock, and examined his wound. It bled profusely both in front and back. The bullet had gone clear through his left shoulder high up, missing the collarbone by the fraction of an inch. Involuntarily Dodge shuddered. A little lower and the wound could very well have been fatal. His predicament was none the less serious. He must try to stop the bleeding somehow. First, however, he wiped his gun dry. Luckily it had not fallen out of the holster. He would need it if whoever had shot him decided to investigate and make sure. There was still no sound of anything moving, so he set about trying to pad the wound and tie his scarf and a strip torn from his shirt around it. It was a makeshift bandage, but it slowed the flow of blood somewhat.

Then Dodge started a laborious climb, mostly on hands and knees, out of the gorge in the direction he believed he had left Baldy. It was slow and painful, and it was not long before he began to feel faint and dizzy. But he kept on. He had to get back to the horse and somehow mount. He would tie himself in the saddle if necessary.

Dodge found he had to rest more often as he climbed higher. He was getting weaker. Once he thought he heard voices. Finally, after a long wait, he attributed this to his imagination. At last he saw the old trail above him, and off to the left the secluded niche where he was sure he would find Baldy. But he had to stop again, and as he lay panting for breath he fought encroaching unconsciousness. Was this, after all, the end? His thoughts were of Nan and how he had utterly failed when he drifted into senselessness.

Some time later he came to. Through hazy vision he saw the figures of two men and horses. One was talking. It was Uncle Bill.

"Wal, Steve, it's lucky fer Dodge here an' us, too, thet you could track a grasshopper. I thought us cattlemen were pretty good, but you backwoods fellars hev us beat."

"We might not hev found him anyway if we hadn't heard the horse raisin' hell. He knew Dodge was close by." It was Steve's voice.

Dodge tried to sit up. He discovered that his wounds were now tightly bound.

"Easy does it, boy," Uncle Bill said. "You jest lay there until we get set to pack you back home. It'll be risky, but not as bad as leavin' you here, or tryin' to stay with you."

"How'd you—ever find me?" Dodge asked.

"Wal, Steve had a hunch you weren't jest lookin' fer cattle, an' we followed your tracks easy until you left the trail. Lucky we picked 'em up again farther down. An' we heard the shot, far off."

"Who shot me?" queried Dodge.

"We found the trail of two horses leadin' west out of the canyon. Steve knew those tracks. It was Hathaway an' his pard Snipe Twitchell. They must hev seen you an' doubled back on foot. We figger Twitchell pulled the trigger. Hathaway's no shucks with a rifle an', ornery as he is, he's not been known to plug a man in the back."

"Snipe—Twitchell. I'll remember that name, Uncle Bill."

"Don't know why he shot high. Snipe doesn't get excited. He's a cussed little sidewinder. Dangerous both with rifle an' six gun, an' lived most of his life here in the Tonto," Steve put in.

"I guess I'm not much good in the deep woods." Dodge smiled weakly.

"Wal, you shore didn't use your haid followin' Hathaway an' Twitchell alone in country they know like the palms of their hands an' where you'd never been," Uncle Bill said bluntly.

"Reckon you were lookin' fer Buck's still," Steve went on. "It ain't up in this canyon. He rides here to meet some friends on top of the Rim."

"Do you know where it is?" asked Dodge.

"Not exactly. I hev a good idee, but—"

"Thet's enough talkin' fer now," Uncle Bill interrupted. "Let's get Dodge home."

Slowly and painfully Dodge was helped to stand erect. He wobbled between them. Then they put him in the saddle.

"Can you stick on?" Uncle Bill's voice was deep with concern.

"Baldy will follow you. I can hang on." Dodge grimaced. "Let's go."

Dodge had been shot before, but never had he experienced the ordeal of that tortuous, long, hard ride back to the Lilleys'. His wound did not bleed, but the pain was agonizing. At dark they tied him in the saddle. Only half-conscious, he leaned over the pommel. Sometime later at night he vaguely remembered being carried to the porch, the sound of muted voices, the touch of soft hands.

CHAPTER 7

It was near the end of August, and Dodge still had not recovered from the bullet wound that had not been very serious in itself, considering other wounds that he had sustained. But in this case infection and inflammation, aggravated by the long and tortuous ride home out of the canyon, had rendered the healing process slow.

His bed had been made at the east end of the porch against the logs and under the window. He could reach out to touch the pine boughs that thrust their tips inside the porch. The day was hot, drowsy, with only the stream murmur and the forest rustle to break the stillness. The hounds were asleep. Moze and Tige, Nan's favorites, had been given the duty of keeping guard over Dodge, a needful precaution in view of the attempt at assassination which had narrowly missed being fatal.

The children were away playing in the woods or paddling in the brook. Only of late had they been permitted to approach Dodge's bedside. What with his illness and their father dying in the cabin they were a subdued and melancholy group of youngsters. Little Rock was the only one who retained much of his initiative during this sad time. Yet it could hardly be said that he did not appreciate the gravity of the situation.

Dodge's fever had left him, so that once more he was aware of what was going on around him. Appetite and reviving energy and interest proved he was on the mend. There had been many moments of late when even his suffering and fever were enjoyed, and these were when Nan dressed his wound and fed him, and sometimes in the dusk knelt beside his bed, whispering things he had not yet been able to believe were more tangible than dreams. It would be pleasant to prolong his stay in bed beyond reason but for the continual reminder that the chief of the Lilleys was near his end. Dodge could hear those horrible hollow rumblings of the backwoodsman's chest, and his raving for the white mule that had so ruthlessly destroyed him. Uncle Bill took it hard. Evidently his devotion to Rock had been lifelong and earnest. Sometimes he sat for a while beside Dodge, in a silent sympathy. But he, like the rest of the household, was waiting. Work, except the duties of the womenfolk, was at a standstill.

The day after Dodge's clash with Hathaway, Ben Lilley had been called before his father, to face a harsh and stormy ordeal. He did not own up to his shortcomings as Steve had done. Later he accused Steve of double-dealing, for which he got knocked down. The bitter quarrel which followed caused an estrangement between the two. Uncle Bill went so far as to say that Hathaway's hold on Ben could not be shaken. Ben rode away and did not return. He was old Rock's second son, Steve being the first.

The other boys had received a shocking lesson and went about with scared, still faces.

So that on this drowsy summer day Dodge had much thought to hold at bay the encroaching gloom. Toward midafternoon the heat subsided and cool, soft breezes came out of the forest, down from the pine-fringed heights. The smell and touch of autumn were in the air, corroborating the flashes of red and gold in the notches of the Rim. The moan of the forest seemed to be for the approaching death of summer. Across the great valley Dodge could see the smoky haze of Indian summer. The heart of nature throbbed on dreamily, indifferent to the lives of men.

Little Rock came up the steps and across the porch, leaving muddy tracks and dripping water in his wake. His big eyes noticed a change in the invalid.

"How air you, Dodge?" he asked.

"Much better, Rock. My fever's gone. I'll be up in a couple of days," replied Dodge.

"I'm orful glad. When you're all well I'll betcha Buck Hathaway ketches hell."

"Rock, why do you pick on Buck?"

"I heard Nan an' Uncle Bill talkin' an' Nan said—"

Here Nan appeared at the window, which opened close to the head of Dodge's bed.

"You, Rock Lilley! I'll tan you good if you go tellin' Dodge tales!" she cried, in wrathful alarm.

From the way in which Rock beat a hasty retreat Dodge inferred that Nan's were not idle threats. It was a hollow-eyed, sad-faced Nan at whom Dodge looked up.

"How's your father?"

"Dad's worse. He can't last long now. Oh, he suffers so. I—I wish he could go quickly."

"Too bad! It hurts me to lie here listening. But I'm most all right, Nan."

"Dodge, I—I'm afraid for you to get well," she said, her big strained eyes bent down upon him. "I almost wish you'd lie here always."

"Well, that's an unkind thought, Nan. But I wouldn't mind so much myself if what I've been dreaming would come true."

"Ravin', you mean. Dodge, you were out of your head," she replied, but color changed the creamy hue of her cheeks.

"Nan, *did* you ever kneel here beside me, in the dark?"

"Yes, every night, and at first, when you were weak from loss of blood, sometimes hours."

"Did you hold my hands?"

"I had to hold *you*—sometimes."

"Lay your face on mine?"

"Y-yes, I reckon."

"And kiss me?"

"I'm afraid I might have. You see I've been out of my head, too."

Dodge gazed up at her a long moment, his heart in his eyes. "Dear Nan, I'll be very sick tonight."

"Yes, you will!" she retorted, and if sorrow had not had too strong a hold she would have laughed. But his suggestion had done its work, he was thrilled to see.

Would she come this night? It seemed a long while to

wait. But, he reflected, if when all had quieted down, and she had not come to him, there was a way to fetch her. The window at the head of his bed opened into the little room where she slept with the children. All he had to do was to pretend he was ill or flighty or even thirsty. And what was innocent pretense in case of love like his? Still, how much sweeter if he did not have to pretend!

The gold died off the Rim and the canyons grew purple. Dusk fell. One of the hounds was up the stream baying a deer. Bats darted to and fro across the sky space between the porch roof and the trees. A burro brayed and a calf bawled.

Nan fetched Dodge's supper rather later than usual. In the dusk under the roof her eyes appeared unnaturally large.

"Nan, I'm as weak as a kitten," he said cheerfully. "You'll have to feed me."

"Oh, dear," sighed Nan, and whether that was further surrender to the inevitable or a complaint of resignation Dodge did not inquire. His appetite certainly was not weak.

"Nan, after everybody is asleep you come out here," he commanded, with most significant tenderness.

"No-o," she faltered.

"If you don't, I'll get up and go prowling around, fall in the brook, maybe be a mark for another bullet, and at least work myself into a fever," he threatened.

"Dodge, how can you be so—so—such a liar?" she exclaimed. "An' it's cruel to torment me now. Do you have to talk to me?"

"Yes."

"What about?"

"Well—everything. At night I lie awake and brood. When I sleep, I dream crazy things. If you'd come to me a little while—"

"But that was when you were out of your head! You're all right now, Dodge."

"Have it your own way then. So if you come it'll be because I want you."

Uncle Bill's slow step announced his approach, which was a signal for Nan's hasty departure.

"Wal, lass, how's this here patient?"

"Very bad, Uncle."

The Texan groped his way in the dusk to find a seat on the box near Dodge's bedside. "How air you, son?"

"Just about well again, Uncle Bill."

"This mawnin' I reckoned you was about ready to rare on Nan. I seen you've bin layin' heah jest to hev her wait on you."

"Fact, Uncle Bill. I could have got up this morning. But, good heavens, how I love that girl!"

"Beats hell—love does! I reckon it's the best thing in life. Only it hurts so. Me an' Rock was kids together. I was older a couple of years, if I recollect. We loved the same girl. An' now he's goin' first. Wal, wal, we don't know jest why things happen as they do."

"Uncle Bill, you think Rock's going soon?"

"Shore. He's daid now to all sense. About midafternoon he had a spell. Then he went different. An' jest before he sunk into it he knew me—said somethin' about Steve an'

Ben. Reckon he may linger on mebbe days. But his agonizin' is over. Pore ole Rock!"

"Steve and Ben! I wonder what was on his mind," Dodge replied.

"Wal, thet ain't hard to guess. Them boys was jest like Rock an' me till Buck Hathaway got them to soakin' up white mule in spite of the fact he won't touch it himself. It gives him a hold over them."

"I guessed as much. Uncle Bill, we've got a strong case against that moonshiner and his white mule."

"To hell with Hathaway! A gun throwed an' he's done with. But thet infernal white mule!"

"Don't worry, old-timer. I scared Steve off it. Sure we ought to work as much for Ben and the other boys."

"Mebbe. If anyone can, you're the man. But somethin' drastic has got to be done, Dodge. I reckon killin' Hathaway ain't enough. All the boys air drinkin' it. Ben's not got the stuff thet's in Steve."

"We'll find the still and smash it up."

"Thet'd be a big help. Mebbe when the boys couldn't get it short of town they might peter off drinkin'."

"Can you buy that drink in the Ryeson saloons?"

"Huh. You shore kin. Two bits a drink."

"It's a sticker, Uncle Bill. How many fine boys have I seen euchered by red liquor! But this white stuff—it must be terrible."

"Dodge, if you touch a match to it, it'll burn. An' I reckon if you'd touch a match to Rock he'd burn as wal."

"Uncle Bill, I want a look at this Snipe Twitchell, out in the open, face to face," said Dodge, changing the subject.

"It's shore a cinch you'll get it, sooner or later. With Hathaway gone it might bust up his outfit, but where he is there you'll find Twitchell. An' you'll hev to kill him."

Dodge felt of the healed wound high up on his shoulder. It was still hot and sore to the touch.

"Uncle Bill, the man doesn't live who could shoot me like that and not meet me later," declared Dodge forcefully.

"Shore, I kin understand thet," agreed Uncle Bill. "I recollect once hearin' Wess Hardin's father—one of the greatest of Texan gunmen—say he'd track a man who shot him in the back around the world to get a look in his eyes."

Dodge grew less communicative after that, and presently Uncle Bill, with a kindly good night, took himself off. Dodge lay there with difficulty shaking off the mood always engendered by this old Texan. An enemy such as this Snipe Twitchell was someone to conjure thoughts which made unpleasant bedfellows.

By and by all sounds ceased within the cabin. Moze and Tige had curled up at the foot of Dodge's bed. A few stars shone through open spaces. The stream murmured on, ever the same; and the night wind sighed fitfully in the forest. Dodge's thoughts had been distracted from the sweet expectancy of a visit from Nan, but when a soft step of a moccasin fell upon his ears he waited, transfixed and thrilling.

She came, almost as silent as a shadow, and sitting beside him on his bed she felt for his hand and slipped hers into it. Used as were his eyes to the darkness he could not make her out clearly; only the dark shape of head and shoulders, and a vague, pale gleam of face with eyes that appeared profound.

"Here I am, Dodge," she whispered simply.

"Thanks, Nan. I—I didn't really expect you," murmured Dodge, with emotion. "But I'm glad you came."

"What'd you want to talk about?"

"It'll come in a moment. Uncle Bill made me sort of gloomy. Tomorrow I'll tell you what he said. But tonight I just wanted to—"

"Yes," she whispered encouragingly, as he hesitated.

"Nan, this is funny," and he laughed under his breath. "Here I've been begging to have you alone with me. Now I've forgotten what I wanted to say."

"It sure couldn't have been very much."

"No! Only that I love you," he retorted, squeezing her hand.

He waited. Her head drooped, and that was the only sign of agitation she betrayed, except possibly a slight trembling of her imprisoned hand. Dodge realized his opportunity, and that now, as always with Nan, he had to be true and direct.

"Nan, I was selfish to coax you out here," he began, in an earnest whisper. "I was hungry for you—to hold your hand like this—to feel you—perhaps to beg a kiss. I had no other reason. I didn't think of—of your dad, of Steve and Ben—of it all. But now that you come I'll give up my selfish desires. I'll tell you this. If you'll promise to be my wife someday I'll be the happiest—the luckiest of men. But if you don't love me—if you can't marry me—I'll stay here anyway, just to help you with your brothers—and to fight for you."

Nan fell on her knees beside his bed and slipping her left arm under his head she hung over him so closely that her hair touched his face.

"Dodge, you're my good angel!"

"That's sweet, Nan. But it's nonsense. I've been a hard-nut range rider. I'm no good angel. I wish to God I could be for you."

"But you are," she insisted softly. "Didn't you upset Buck Hathaway's plans? Didn't you expose this white-mule deal? Didn't you wake Steve to where he was headin'?"

"All so little, Nan. I don't deserve your grand opinion."

"Didn't you hear me tap on the log that Sunday night—after your fight with Buck?"

"Did you? I thought I'd dreamed that."

"I did tap. One—two—then, after a while—three!"

"Who's the angel now?" he returned thickly, fighting to prolong the sweetness of this moment.

"Listen, you doubtin' Dodge. You took my very breath that day by the brook. I fell terribly in love with you. But I didn't know—an' I wasn't free to tell you till that Sunday night."

"Oh, Nan, then you *do* love me?"

"Dodge, I used to laugh about love for anyone outside our family. And about the way it was always drummed into my ears how the Lilleys loved. Oh, dear! It's sure no laughin' matter. When I found out it was you, I just gave up. Then I'd shake at the sound of your step. I'd watch you from a distance. I yearned for you to drag me off into the woods and make me give away my love. I used to brush against you when waiting on you at table—brazen little hussy that I was! Look innocent when I was horribly guilty. Then, those first days after you were shot, I used to hang over you for hours. At night I'd come here, like this, and when you were out of your head, I'd kiss you and love you till I had no more strength. Now!"

"*Nan!* This is only another crazy nightmare of mine," he cried, beside himself.

"No, Dodge, you're sure not dreamin'. This is reality for us. I'm here on my knees by your bed. You've been shot in the back—almost murdered. My dad lies dyin' inside there. Ben has gone off to his ruin. Oh, it's no dream. It's terrible trouble—all too true!"

"For God's sake, don't be sad at this moment!" he entreated. "Make my dream come true."

"What shall I do? Man alive, haven't I told you?"

"Nan, could you do now while I'm conscious what you did when I was raving and didn't know?"

"I reckon I—might," she whispered, bending lower over him until her dark image blotted out the stars. Her arm slid farther around him.

"Well?"

"Provided I tell you one more thing—that settles us forever."

"Then hurry."

"I do love you, Dodge. And I'll be your wife as soon as you want—after Dad is gone."

Dodge drew her down to him and spent all his passion

of love and gratitude upon her lips, cheeks, and eyes. Then, releasing her abruptly, he let her slip back to her knees.

"Go to bed, Nan darling," he whispered huskily. "Leave me here to lie awake thinking how to be worthy of you and how to serve you and yours."

CHAPTER 8

Two days later Rock Lilley passed on to his last account The suspense of the Lilleys had its outburst in grief. Ruthless and iron he had been to his family, yet he had been worshiped by them. They gave him a pioneer burial under the junipers where the gravestones of his mother and two of his offspring stood.

Ben Lilley did not come home, a fact over which Uncle Bill gravely shook his head. Steve, as the eldest son, took his father's place in the affairs of family and ranch. To Dodge's offer to buy cattle enough to become a partner in the ranch Steve said: "I'll shore be glad to, Dodge, if Hathaway does not take our land an' stock away from us."

"Buck won't get quite so much land as this," replied Dodge, with enigmatical mildness.

"About six foot, I reckon," drawled Uncle Bill.

"Oh, you men!" cried Nan impatiently. "But *can* Hathaway take our ranch from us?"

"For what?" queried Steve darkly.

"White mule he sold to Dad. He gave his word. The word of a Lilley!"

"Nan, that deal would not hold in any court," interposed Dodge quickly. "You forget that the distilling of moonshine whisky is against the law."

"But Dad's word has nothin' to do with the law. Steve, you're head of the Lilleys now. You should give up the ranch."

"I never gave my word, Nan," replied Steve stoutly.

"Dad's is ours," went on Nan gravely. "Let us pay. You and Dodge can homestead somewhere else in the valley. Sure Tess and I will help."

"Uncle Bill, what do you say? I reckon Nan's right."

"Shore, Nan's right. I'd back her agin anythin'. But all the same I don't see the sense in givin' your all to a man as good as dead," drawled the Texan.

Nan cast a swift glance from her uncle to Dodge, and her face turned pale.

"I hate to oppose you, dear," said Dodge quietly, "but I stand by Uncle Bill."

"Steve, s'pose you an' Nan wait till Hathaway makes a move," added the Texan.

"That's easy. Will you agree to that, Nan? Let's wait."

With this issue laid aside for the present the Lilleys approached something of the easy tenor of their ways. The womenfolk set about many neglected tasks and the boys went into the fields. Significant indeed was it that the hogs and horses were turned into the sorghum field. Dodge devoted himself to getting stronger. He did not need Uncle Bill's grave advice or Nan's pleading eyes and lips to make him careful about how he exposed himself. He had the eyes of a hawk and the ears of a deer. Only

[100]

Uncle Bill suspected what was on Dodge's mind, and, like the true Texan he was, he never let a chance go by to add fuel to the smouldering flame.

Then suddenly, like a bolt out of a clear sky, came a shock worse than old Rock's death. Elmer Lilley returned from Ryeson, a distracted boy, raving so violently that it took patience to get his story. Ben had been killed by Buck Hathaway.

They had all, except Uncle Bill, believed Ben would come home to make up with Steve. He had been easily led, weak under the influence of liquor, but when he was himself the mildest and most cheerful of boys.

After the first horror of the fact of Ben's death had been realized they got Elmer calmed enough to talk.

"It was in front of Ryan's. They'd all been inside drinkin' ceptin' Buck. They was arguin' too. I was jest by the door listenin' an' tryin' to git a chance to tell Ben about Pa. Reckoned he might not hev heard," Elmer related. "Ben was complainin' to Buck about money. Said he wasn't gettin' enough. Finally Ben got up from the table whar they was sittin' and give Buck some partin' words. He said, 'Mebbe it'd be worth more to some other folks fer me to tell what I know about you an' yore outfit, Buck. Includin' the whereabouts of yore still.' With that Ben turned his back and walked out. I saw Twitchell whisper somethin' to Buck."

Elmer stopped to get his breath. "Wal, you know Ben had taken to packin' a gun. I slipped out the door behind him aimin' to call to him. But jest then Buck follered him an' hollered, 'So you're goin' to turn yeller an' slink back home, you would-be bad man.' Ben sort of turned white an' started to answer. Then he jerked at thet big gun, an' Hathaway shot him. Ben didn't hev a chance. It was murder. I'd hev bet he was through with thet outfit an' meant to come home. An'— I guess there ain't no more to tell."

With that brief and to-the-point recital Elmer Lilley strode off toward the woods.

"Dodge, you an' Uncle Bill come out with me—away from the cabin," said Steve somberly. "The rest of you stay home an' wait fer us."

Dodge saw the Lilley temper of the lad as he had seen it in Nan. Steve was as white as marble and his eyes had a singularly piercing light, as hard as ice. He halted out under the pines.

"Uncle Bill, an' you, pard Dodge, cain't see this here deal any way but my way," he cried ringingly.

"An' what's that, son?" queried Uncle Bill.

"No more can go on here till Buck Hathaway is dead."

"Wal, you said a heap. How about it, Dodge?" replied the old Texan coolly.

"My God, it never should have gone so far!" exclaimed Dodge indignantly. "Why didn't I shoot that coyote when I had the chance?"

"Ahuh. I'm remindin' you about sayin' that very thing. Too late!"

"I'm sorry. Steve, it was only for Nan's sake. I love her. I hated to have her see me kill Hathaway. I'll make up for it—damned pronto!"

"Dodge, it's too late fer that," rejoined Steve, his brows

knitted. "I'll kill Hathaway. It's my job. Dad would expect it. Even Nan will sanction it."

"Wal, Steve, I agree. A Lilley has got to kill thet lousy moonshiner. If *I* hev to do it myself!" Uncle Bill's reply was uncompromising.

Dodge stood sunk in deep thought. He had been quick to grasp Steve's point of view, his respect for a creed. And now his swift mind was evolving ways and means to help the lad.

"Listen, both of you," he said suddenly. "I've got another gun like this in my bag, and a lot of shells. I'll teach Steve to throw that gun quick. Like this! Then after he has the knack of a swift draw he can practice real shooting, until I see he's good for it. And he can go after Hathaway."

"I'm good fer that now. I can beat Buck any day."

"But let's make shore," put in Uncle Bill persuasively. "You've Tess to think of, an' Nan, an' all the kids. Why'n hell should you take even a little risk?"

"How long will it take to satisfy you I'm good fer the job? demanded Steve. "This here is somethin' I won't wait long fer."

Dodge unloaded his gun, and taking off his belt he fastened it on Steve.

"There. Shove the gun back. Now, place your hands natural. Then draw—quick as hell!"

Steve had a deadly look as he complied, and his action had remarkable celerity.

"Dodge, he ain't so slow," ejaculated the grim old Texan, very much pleased.

"If you hadn't stopped a second to cock the gun, you'd have done well. That might have done for Hathaway. He's a killer, cold-blooded and mean. But I did not need to be told he can't throw a gun. Now, watch me. When I grab the gun, my thumb is there, on the hammer. I jerk the gun out—in fact throw it as if I was going to throw it at you. The weight and force throw the gun down to a level. They flip the hammer from under my thumb. That discharges the gun. There's nothing else to gun-throwin'— except practice. Now watch!"

Dodge gave several examples to illustrate what he had been explaining.

"Do it slow. I can't see what you do or how you do it. Shore I get yore hunch. But show me—slow!"

Steve was white and moist of face. His gaze held a terrible eager intensity.

Whereupon Dodge executed his draw in action that Steve could comprehend and the better learn to imitate.

"Ahuh. So thet's what it means to be King Fisher an' Wess Hardin', not to speak of my Kansas-ridin' pard. By Gawd! Gimme back thet gun an' go get the one you'll lend me. Uncle Bill, the lousy moonshiner who killed pore old Dad is as good as dead!"

The younger Lilley boys packed Ben's body on a horse up from Ryeson, and buried him in a grave prepared by Dodge and Uncle Bill. Although Steve and the womenfolk were conspicuous by their absence it was no less a grievous occasion. Uncle Bill considered it still more of a lesson for the younger Lilleys.

Reliable information and also gossip brought back from

Ryeson by Uncle Bill only added fuel to the flame of resentment toward Hathaway. Such a malignant character as his was far from new to Dodge, who had seen so many bad men come and go on the Kansas ranges. But it seemed that Buck Hathaway had earned his evil repute only of recent months. Other Hathaways in the valley repudiated any connection with him. Something had imbued him with hate.

The old Texan concluded his report: "He's grown as sore as a shed rattler. He swears now he'll ride up here an' drive us Lilleys off Rock's ranch."

"He will, like the old lady who kept tavern out West," replied Dodge tartly.

"Haw! Haw! All the same, Dodge, I'm not likin' the whole damn situation. Let's git a move on."

It was late afternoon and Dodge was sitting on his bed while Uncle Bill utilized the bench. They were waiting for a call to supper and imagined they were alone.

"We'll move all right, soon as Steve is up to the job he swears is his," Uncle Bill said after a silence.

Suddenly Nan was leaning out of her window, and she put her hands down around Dodge's neck to lay hold of his coat.

"Ahuh! So that's what Steve is up to?" she demanded.

Dodge had only had a glimpse of her tragic face, and now he was imprisoned so that he could not see her. After his start and settling back he was just as well satisfied. Uncle Bill readily attempted to retrieve the error.

"Don't lie, Uncle," retorted Nan shortly. "Steve has sure been queer lately. An' I saw him with a big gun like

Dodge's. Today there's been shootin' all day way off in the woods. Now it's easy to put two an' two together. Steve is goin' to meet Hathaway."

Dodge felt caught in more ways than by these firm, tender hands, and Uncle Bill let out a snort that meant surrender. Neither, evidently, had a word to say.

"Dodge, if Buck Hathaway kills Steve too, I'll never get over it," went on Nan.

Then Dodge gripped her hands and blurted out: "Nan, the chances will be all Steve's."

"Still, if you're honest you'll admit Steve might fail. He's only nineteen. Even if he is a Lilley he might not live up to it, in a pinch. Buck is a man. He's had several shootin' frays an' when he's in a rage he's a perfect devil."

There was a silence fraught with considerable suspense. In addition to her grave, eloquent words Dodge had the feel of her hands to contend with. And they were all-convincing.

Uncle Bill burst out: "Thet's jest the hell of it, Nan. Steve wouldn't hear of Dodge takin' this cause as his. We had to give in."

"Sure, I understand. But were you right to do so? I've stood a lot, Dodge. I can't stand much more. Is it good judgment lettin' Steve risk this? I love you terribly an' my heart just chokes me when I think of you meetin' Hathaway. But my sense tells me he could never be smart enough or quick enough to kill you."

Dodge kissed her hands one after the other.

"Nan, I deserve that rebuke," he said. "There's hardly any excuse for me. But I've been so scared of you Lilleys.

First you, then your dad, and now Steve! I can't explain just what I did feel. Forget it now and stop your worrying."

A call to supper ended that scene, and when Dodge saw Nan again she appeared pale and cool, surely with less tension of face and less troubled eyes. After supper she came to him where he sat on the porch rail watching the gold fade off the promontory.

"Dodge, I forgot to tell you somethin'," she whispered. "Tess will be here Sunday, an' sure as you're born she'll see through Steve. She'll go wild. She'll break his nerve. She couldn't keep Steve from meeting Buck, no more'n I, but she'd sure hurt his chances. Tess is only a kid. Why, she gets scared when Steve goes bear hunting."

"Gosh, I'd like to have a sweetheart who'd go wild over me," replied Dodge lightly.

"Much you know about women, Dodge Mercer!" retorted Nan, with an unfathomable glance, and though he endeavored to detain her she broke free and ran. And later it was Bess, the next eldest of the Lilley girls, who furnished Dodge with the biscuits, meat, and salt he wanted for his saddlebags.

CHAPTER 9

Next morning at dawn Dodge was surprised to meet Uncle Bill at the barn saddling a horse. A blanket and rifle lay on a stump.

"Mawnin', Dodge. Was you goin' somewheres again?" he asked facetiously.

"Howdy, old-timer, guess I was," replied Dodge with a laugh.

"Wal, this time you ain't goin' alone. Besides, I reckon I know about whar thet moonshine still is," he said significantly. "We might as well make a call down thar on our way to wherever you was headin'."

"Lead on, Uncle Bill. You caught me in the act so you lead the party." Dodge laughed again. He had been with Texans before. They rode off together into the forest, munching a scant breakfast in the saddle.

The sun had not risen, though the black fringe of the Rim was changing to rose. Frost showed on stumps and peeled logs, and the purple maples, the red sumach; the bronze and green sycamores attested to the arrival of autumn.

They followed the stream trail down to lower country, where the pines failed and the richness of the forest ceased. Soon the stream entered a brush-walled gully, which grew gradually into the proportions of a canyon. Wild turkey and deer fled before the steady clip-clop of the horses.

"Here's where we climb," announced the Texan, pointing to a yellow wall opposite. They crossed the amber stream for the last time and took to a zigzag trail up a dusty oak-thicketed ridge, and climbed up into the sunshine, and higher, to a point where Dodge began to see the bold Bald Ridges. But soon that view was lost and Dodge had a long, hot ride up and down, and always walled in by scrub oak and manzanita and cactus. Then they mounted by a roundabout way to cedar and piñon groves, out of which they rode at last upon a rocky, scaly bare ridge that appeared to wind and slope for miles down into a blue void. Beyond this and above rose the bald faces of higher ridges that wound and sloped down from the opposite direction.

Dodge was riding into the country which from far above had struck him so forcibly. Next to the singular bare ridges what affected him most was the size of the country. These ridges were miles long, and the gorges between were wide and deep, and both sloped down into a dark, bronze-walled fastness.

Uncle Bill saw the country from a different point of view.

"Hell of a range fer stock, but jest look at the grass,"

he remarked. "This here was Rock's range till Hathaway got it."

"Say, you could run ten thousand head of cattle here!" ejaculated Dodge, amazed.

"Shore. An', Dodge, right here I'll spring my idee on you. Let's me an' you throw in with the Lilleys. Steve an' Nan will be strong fer it. I'll go home an' close out my cattle bizness. Come back an' take root fer good."

"Hits me right," said Dodge heartily. "I've some money, enough to start in with a hundred head. Old-timer, it's a great idea. I can see us developing a great cattle range."

"Shore. An' rustlers, too. But we can train these six Lilley boys—no, only five, by Gawd! There's a fortune here, Dodge."

"Yes, with drawbacks. First we must start getting rid of Hathaway and his outfit. Then we've got to finish by getting rid of the other outfits as they come along. Sheepmen will come, sure."

"Hell, yes! I kin see a big fight between sheepmen an' cattlemen here in years to come. But we're first, an' we kin fix the Lilleys fer life. What do you say, Dodge?"

"Shake on it, old-timer."

An hour later the riders were as far down this ridge as their horses could carry them. Dodge felt that it was indeed the jumping-off place. Far above, the yellow ramparts curved into the blue. And down here on three sides canyons yawned—the main one, still far below, a rent in bronze walls, and to left and right thicket-spotted, red-cragged, steep broken slopes of gorges the bottoms of which could not be seen.

"It's down here somewhar," announced the Texan, wiping his sweaty face. "This is Saturday, an' thet's shore the day Hathaway an' his outfit go to town to collect an' gamble. Any day but today an' Sunday you shore kin see blue smoke comin' out of here. So let's go down, Dodge, an' get this sweaty job done."

"Don't you reckon there's a trail leading down? Else how could all that sorghum be packed in?"

"Shore. Thet trail must come down the gully. We came by short cut, accordin' to Steve's direction."

Farther descent was so difficult as to be precarious. It was almost perpendicular. But for brush and broken rock they would have slid down. However, in a short time they stood in a narrow, dry stream bed along the margin of which ran a well-defined trail. Dodge bent to scrutinize horse tracks.

"Two days old an' more," he said. "I reckon we've hit the right time, Bill."

"Shore. But I hit the wrong place to come down. This is a boulevard."

"Go slow and step soft. If there's any surprise party we want it to be ours."

Cautiously they made slow progress down the gorge. It narrowed to a dark defile and opened out into a wide little valley, riotous with the scarlet and gold of autumn leaves. Deer bounding away lent conviction to the probability that the place was deserted on this day. The oak thickets were covered with acorns and bear tracks were numerous.

"Here we air, an' nobody home," announced the Texan

with satisfaction, and he pointed to a roofed shed under the right wall. "It ain't a big camp. Wonder now if Hathaway hasn't got another still somewhere."

They approached and soon found what they sought. No precautions had been taken to hide the still. Evidently its owner considered the remote canyon a sufficient hiding place. Its coils and tanks had a snaky, ominous look. Dodge's purpose was to destroy. The larger shelter contained several beds, stacks of sorghum, sacks full of grain, shelves of food supplies, an open fireplace and chimney, a rude table and benches, and lastly a neat storage of brown jugs, similar to the one Rock Lilley had proffered to Dodge on the occasion of his welcome.

"Wal, Dodge, will you hev a taste of white mule, just fer luck?" spoke up Bill dryly.

Dodge turned to see him with a jug in hand and a grim grin on his rugged face.

"Here's to Buck Hathaway! May he make plenty of white mule in hell!" He drank and let out a cough like that of a choking horse.

"Old-timer, I'll taste it, so as to be in on your toast," replied Dodge, and took the jug. A second later he flung it from him with a crash.

"Haw! Haw! It's shore funny what thet stuff makes you look like. But thar's nuthin' funny about the way it makes you feel."

"Waugh! Didn't mean to swallow any, but it slid down my throat. Come on, Bill, let's bust things."

"Wade in, son, an' think of Rock."

Dodge picked up a sledge and with a few tremendous

blows smashed the still to ruins. How strange to see that even the ruins seemed to hold the same menace.

"Thet'll be about all," drawled the old Texan, and Dodge, turning, saw that he had set fire to the larger shelter.

Dodge swung his leg across his saddle and gazed from the divide down across the Bald Ridges. A column of yellow smoke rose above the canyons to mushroom and billow away on the wind.

"No forest-fire smoke, that's shore," said old Bill. "I reckon every man in the basin will see an' do some tall reckonin'."

"It has a queer look, that smoke," agreed Dodge.

"Wal, Hathaway's gang will be wise," declared Bill. "An' it's shore strikin' flint over powder. Dodge, did you get the same hunch down thar as me?" queried the old Texan, pointing down into the smoke-curtained gorge.

"I can't say I got any hunch," replied Dodge slowly. "I was too full of glee."

"Wal, I reckon you don't know much about moonshine stills. That one we've just wiped out hadn't been worked lately. An' it was far too small to turn out all the white mule Hathaway distributes around."

"Aha! Your hunch was that that outfit runs a bigger still?"

"Exactly. Did you take a peek at that pile of sorghum?"

"Yes," replied Dodge.

"Did it look like what we raise up under the Rim?"

"Bill, I couldn't say."

"Wal, we never raised it, that's shore. All the sorghum

Hathaway packed out of our fields went somewhere else. We can gamble there's another an' bigger one."

"Gosh! That complicates the deal. Hathaway's outfit will lay low. It'll take a fight to destroy another one."

"Huh! We got to find it first. An' there's goin' to be a fight anyhow."

After that the two men rode in silence down the winding trail. Once down off the Bald Ridges they entered the heavy growth of pine, cedar, and piñon. This belt gradually thinned out, the pines failed, and open sunny patches took the places of cool shade. Sumach was reddening on the rocky slopes. At length they reached a road, which eventually led down out of the hills into a wide flat where the yellowing foliage of walnut trees contrasted markedly with a soil of bare reddish sand. The flat was evidently a swale bisected by a dry stream bed. Dodge was the first to see the horsemen entering the flat from the opposite side.

"Steve—or I'm jiggered!" exclaimed old Bill. "Now I just wonder who's that ridin' with him."

Presently the horsemen met at a point where a huge walnut tree spread a colorful shade across the road. Dodge was quick to see that Steve appeared gloomy and hard. His companion was a striking, dark-skinned man who held Dodge's attention.

"Wal, Steve, here you are. Me an' Dodge was trailin' you. Howdy, Coplace. Ain't seen you fer a spell. Where you bound, son?"

"I was ridin' in to meet Hathaway," spoke up Steve quickly. "Figgered maybe you were tryin' to beat me to it," he said, looking directly at Dodge. "But I run into Coplace here. An' he talked me out of goin'. We're old huntin' pards, Dodge. Shake hands with Jim Coplace. Jim, this is the friend I was tellin' you about."

Coplace's instant response and iron grip added to Dodge's first favorable impression.

"Glad to meet any pard of Steve's," he said frankly. "The boy needs them along about now."

"Humph! Talked a Lilley out of somethin', hey? Wal, that shore requires palaverin'," interposed old Bill. "Let's git off in the shade an' hear all about it."

The four horsemen dismounted. Dodge tied Baldy to a cedar bush. Upon his return to the trio he ran an appreciative glance over Coplace's lithe, powerful figure. The man was undoubtedly part Indian, and when Dodge saw him sit down cross-legged he was sure of it. Dodge took off his sombrero and vest and wiped his moist face. He became aware of Coplace's close scrutiny.

"Wal, talk, cain't you?" spoke up the old Texan irritably.

"Uncle, you know how Dad was against my huntin' with Jim?"

"Somethin' about it, lad. But I never took much stock in that. Rock swore Coplace stole a bar hound from him."

"I never did," denied Coplace, with a grin at Dodge. "The hound came to my camp and wouldn't leave."

"That's no matter now," went on Steve. "But I wanted you both to know Jim an' I have been huntin' pards just the same."

"All right with me," declared Bill heartily.

"Jim was ridin' out home to give us Lilleys a hunch,"

said Steve, drawing a deep breath. His eyes were somber. Dodge divined that the boy had faced some bitter obstacle to his feud with Hathaway.

"Wal, thet's good of you, Coplace," drawled Bill. "Just how far can we take thet?"

"Old man, there's going to be hell under the Rim an' I'm on the Lilleys' side," replied Coplace.

"Ahuh. Thet ain't so bad fer us to hear," drawled the Texan coolly. "What have you agin Hathaway?"

"My mother is an Apache. Only a few of my family left. Hathaway sells white mule to them."

Dodge gauged the half-breed's intelligence and character from that speech. Then he took particular note of Coplace's dark eagle cast of face, his piercing eyes, his muscular build, and half-buckskin garb he wore, the way he carried knife and gun in his belt, and the Winchester in his saddle sheath. The sum of these observations, added to his intuitive judgment of the caliber of a man, convinced him that Steve had an exceedingly valuable friend and the Hathaway contingent a dangerous enemy.

"Coplace, how come you took so much on your shoulders?" asked the old Texan curtly.

"Steve couldn't have got an even break," rejoined the half-breed.

"Wal, thet's new for Ryeson. I remember a good many fellars—an' some with lots of enemies—who had an even break. Ryeson's always been a square shootin' place."

"No more. You know what happened to Ben. Hathaway's gatherin' his clan an' means to do away with all the Lilleys," replied Coplace darkly.

"*Clan!*" ejaculated old Bill.

Dodge repeated the word with scarcely less astonishment.

"Uncle Bill, you an' Dodge listen," spoke up Steve, throwing off restraint. "When I met Jim down here a ways he was ridin' out home to give us a hunch. An' here it is. Hathaway got it straight from all friends of the Lilleys what he might expect. He'd have to kill Dodge an' me an' all of us men if he wanted to stay in the Tonto. Somebody has got a line on Dodge an' spread it around. Thet upset the Hathaway outfit. Accordin' to Jim here, all that is town talk."

"Wal, son, thet ain't nuthin' to upset us," replied old Bill.

"I reckon not. But it's only a little. Now it chanced that Jim was trailin' a hawse back of his homestead, which is up on the cedar bench above Ryeson. An' Jim came on a camp back in Turkey Creek scarce a mile from town. It's a thick, brushy cover. He slipped up to see who was there. An' he was plumb surprised to recognize Snipe Twitchell and the three Quayle brothers. They didn't have any packs, which showed the camp wasn't permanent. They was waitin' for someone, an' Jim gambled it was Hathaway. So he just lay low an' waited. It was along late in the afternoon. Some time after sundown Hathaway showed up on foot, packin' some grub an' a jug fer the boys. This was no first meetin', Jim claims. But it was shore enthusiastic. After it got dark Jim crawled close enough to hear what it was all about. Tellin' it short an' sweet, they're organizin' to kill or drive off us Lilleys. Accordin' to Jim they shore divided things among themselves. Hathaway wants Nan an' means to have her by hook or crook. Twitchell aims at the Lilley ranch, an' the Quayle brothers agreed on one of Hathaway's moonshine stills as their share. An' that's about all."

A blank silence ensued. Dodge glanced from the pale Steve to Coplace, who chewed grass stems and bent his eyes upon the sand. Old Bill showed perturbation, but it was slowly rising wrath.

"Who are the Quayles?" asked Dodge, keen to get this situation in hand.

"Mostly the last of a bad-egg family from Missouri," replied Bill. "There was five sons, the ole man, an' some cousins—a tough outfit, even fer hereabouts. Rock told me once thet old Reub Quayle was not the rulin' element. Anyway, he an' the two oldest boys got shot over in Pleasant Valley. They was hawse thieves proper. The three younger boys stayed away from Ryeson since. I don't know what became of the rest. We heard of them now an' then. Nothin' good."

"This Snipe Twitchell who shot me—tell me more about him," went on Dodge.

"Wal, I reckon you'd call Snipe the only hombre in the outfit who is dangerous—that is to a man of your stripe. He's got nerve an' he can handle a gun. An' he's the last of the Twitchells. Was only a boy when the Twitchell clan got wiped out. I reckon Snipe an' the Quayles are related."

"Coplace, what's your idea of the way this clan will work?" asked Dodge finally.

"Not out in the open. But Twitchell wouldn't back away

from no man, or he'd shoot from ambush, as you know. We'll have to keep off the trails an' under cover."

"Wal, I reckon we'll hunt them instead of waitin' to be hunted," drawled old Bill.

"That would be my idea," interposed Coplace.

"But that'd leave Nan an' our ranch for them to grab," said Steve anxiously.

"We'll take Nan with us," suggested Dodge.

"Good idee, by gum," declared Bill, slapping his knee. "Steve, I reckon we ought to elect Dodge head of the Lilley clan."

"No. I don't feel equal to that responsibility—not against a bunch of backwoodsmen. Coplace is our best bet."

"I reckon so, too, Uncle Bill," agreed Steve.

"Suits me," replied the Texan. "But before we git down to figgerin' let me tell you thet Dodge an' me put one of Hathaway's stills out of commission."

"You did! By heaven, thet's good! Jim saw yellow smoke risin' out of the canyons. We shore wondered."

"Steve, this still was up near where the canyons head. It was a small one, an' hadn't been worked much lately. Thar's a big moonshine mill somewhar."

"Hathaway keeps thet place secret," rejoined Steve.

"I can track sorghum packers without gettin' off my horse," said Coplace contemptuously.

"Wal, I reckoned the very same thing," spoke up old Bill, rubbing his hands. "Now what'll we do?"

Coplace smoked out his cigarette. Then he said: "Got plenty of loads?" And tapped his gun significantly.

"Wal, we ain't so stocked up on forty-fours as I'd like. Reckon we'll be usin' Winchesters," replied old Bill.

Coplace got up. "I'll ride back to Ryeson. Take a heap a look round. Gimme money to buy shells for your forty-fours. My rifle shoots the same. Nobody will guess I'm in the Lilley outfit yet. I'll come to the ranch tomorrow. You go home an' keep off trails. Put hounds out all night. Watch sharp."

With that he untied his ragged horse, and mounting rode off under the trees toward the high ground. The men watched him disappear.

"Steve, I got a hunch your half-Indian pard is a whole outfit for us," said Dodge.

"Huh! I guess. Why, Dodge, he's the wonderfulest man in the woods you ever saw. Shoots runnin' turkeys in the neck. With a rifle! Jim is a queer one. No friends among the whites. But he isn't understood. I happened to come on him sick in a camp up here. An' I fetched him grub an' medicine. We got to be friends. My Gawd! how lucky for us Lilleys. He hates Hathaway an' he hates white mule!"

"Wal, by gum, it's shore been a bad day for the Hathaway clan," declared old Bill. "Come, let's rustle."

CHAPTER 10

Steve led straight for the foothills, and once in them gave an open-range rider like Dodge a taste of brushy travel.

There were no trails and seldom an open patch of ground and never a level. The red sand hills were thickly covered with manzanita, mescal, scrub oak, and other brush hard on horse and man. Knolls gave place to mounds and mounds to hills, and these led steeply upward to a long, green slope topped with white outcroppings of limestone. This, Dodge learned, was the face of Limestone Mesa. Once having surmounted that, Dodge saw a wide level plateau, sparsely timbered near the edge but growing dense with cedar, piñon, and juniper, which in turn led into the zone of pines. Far above towered the golden-belted, black-fringed Rock Rim that dominated the country.

Cattle and wild horses were numerous but scarcely as numerous as the deer. Birds and small game were abundant. A rocky gulch split the plateau, and a swift, amber-colored brook delighted Dodge's eye. Wild turkeys, scattered into the green. Steve led into a well-defined trail and here the horses made up for slow travel. In open places Dodge looked back and down. It appeared that the farther up he climbed the more rough and inaccessible that Bald Ridge country looked. Yellow smoke still rose from a dark crooked line of canyon.

This day had given Dodge a good idea of a section of what they called the Tonto Basin. He failed to see where the name "Basin" was felicitous. Perhaps the whole hollow encompassed by rim and mountains was what had been named. Anyway, Dodge felt like tipping his sombrero to the wildest, roughest, and most beautiful country he had ever ridden.

Sunset caught the riders at an abandoned ranch. A tumbledown log cabin and acres of cleared land growing up in weeds, brush, and sumach attested to the futile labors of some pioneer.

From this point to the cleared sections belonging to the Lilleys was only a short ride. Dodge recognized the bare fields, the plots of corn still uncut, the ghastly dead pines standing here and there in the open, and lastly, far across the open, the roof of the big cabin peeping out of the forest. Long before the riders reached the heavy fence of poles old Rock's bear hounds made the welkin ring. They rode up to a porch lined by the anxious faces of Steve's family.

"Here we are, hungrier'n a parcel of bar dogs," shouted old Bill, genially.

Dodge caught a glimpse of Nan's glad face and then the gleaming eyes of her brothers.

"Pile off an' throw leather," called Bill. "We'll let the hawses loose in the yard."

Then in a lower voice he instructed Dodge to tell Nan of the latest developments, Steve to do likewise with his brothers, Denton and George, while he prepared Mrs. Lilley for what might happen.

"Wal, you gun-packin' son of a gun, I see you're home," said little Rock, as Dodge wearily climbed the high steps. The lad's dry tone and keen, bright look brought a laugh from the rider. Rock was a chip off the old block.

"Howdy, son. Sure I'm back home and darn glad to see you all," replied Dodge cheerfully.

"D'je bore thet—anybody?" inquired the youngster.

"No, Rock. Saw some turkeys, but they was moving too fast."

"Turkeys my eye!" quoth Rock in disgust.

"Boy, get me a pan of water, soap, and a towel. I'm plumb black from that ride. Your brother Steve can sure hit the brush."

A little later Dodge was called to supper. Afterward he talked with Bill and Steve. They agreed that they could only wait and watch until Coplace came. The children were put to bed. Steve went off with his brothers, and Bill sought Mrs. Lilley inside the cabin. Dodge was enjoying a rest and a quiet smoke in the huge rustic chair where Rock had sat so often when Nan came out in the shadow. She promptly sat down on his lap, gave him a quick kiss, and dropped her head with a sigh on his shoulder.

"Gosh, it's terrible to love somebody," she whispered.

"Anybody?"

"Yes—anybody. Dodge, when I saw you I was so glad my heart just quit on me."

"Mine flopped up an' down a bit. But I wouldn't change my place with any man on earth."

"Now?" she asked softly.

"Now or hereafter."

"Oh, dear! Dodge, suppose you act a little more like a lover before you spring new trouble on me."

Dodge laughed and quickly made up for his neglect. Then he told her in detail the events of the day.

"Denton saw the smoke down over the canyons. So you burned out the lousy moonshiner. Dodge, it was a bad day for Hathaway when you met me by the brook."

"Dear, I reckon it was. But this clan war, as Steve called it, seems to complicate the deal."

"It doesn't scare me as much as you an' Steve goin' out alone to meet him."

"Old Bill says with the Indian Coplace on our side that this new-baked clan of Hathaway won't have a ghost of a show."

"I've heard Dad tell about Coplace. Wonderful hunter. Dad was jealous of him. But oh, no matter if you had all the Apaches left in the valley, I'd still worry my heart out while you're away. It'll be worse now, Dodge. I won't be safe."

"Dearest, I won't be away from you any more."

"What?" queried Nan, lifting her head.

"We are not going to be separated. According to what Coplace heard, Hathaway's plan is to get you by hook or crook. So you are going to ride with us."

"Dodge! You'll—take me?" gasped Nan.

"Yes. You'll run less risk with us. So, my sweetheart, you shall wear a man's togs, ride hard, sleep hard, fare hard, and shoot hard, too, if I don't mistake your Lilley temper. Have you got a riding outfit?"

"Sure have."

"A rifle?"

"Yes. Winchester forty-four. Carbine length. I can shoot it, too, Mister Abilene Dodge."

"Oh, you can? Well, what can you hit?"

"Your sombrero five times out of six shots at a hundred yards."

"Fair. How about say three hundred yards?"

"I could sure hit a man," replied Nan, with a grim little note in her voice.

"If you had a chance to draw down on Hathaway, would you?" queried Dodge curiously.

"Would I!" Then she shuddered. "Oh, Dodge, it's sickening—what I feel. I'd be wretched all my life, I suppose. But if I ever get a bead on—"

"I hope you don't," interrupted Dodge, squeezing her. "The chances are that Coplace will do for that hombre. Nan, we may ride out tomorrow. You must figure what you'll need. I can help you."

"Darlin', it'll likely end in my helpin' you. Don't forget we're backwoods folks an' this is the Tonto. You rode away this morning without saddlebags. You should have packed cooked meat or dried beef, salt, jerky, dried apples, parched corn, a sack of biscuits."

"Ex—cuse me, Miss Lilley. I'm happy to see that my future wife will never let me ride away to starve."

"Oh, Dodge—don't—don't make fun," she cried, shrinking to him with a little sob. "I may be a Lilley, but I—I'm only a girl. Your future wife! Oh, will I ever be?"

"Nan, I've faced many more dangerous propositions than this Hathaway one. They'll outnumber us. But with Coplace we have a great advantage. Twitchell is the only one of that outfit to consider seriously."

"Those Quayle brothers! I remember Ruby an' Diamond Quayle. Funny names for boys. They're twins. You can't tell them apart. They were at a dance a year before I went to Texas. Handsome devils. I had to be taken home on their account."

"My Nan, these Quayle admirers of yours may be handy after girls and breaking up dances, but I think you can discount them against men like Steve's half-breed and your humble cowboy from the Panhandle."

"You make me creep. Dodge, you have that edge on your voice—when you first called Hathaway. Oh, Dodge dear, kiss me, let me be a girl just once more."

In the morning Dodge was awakened by squirrels frisking about under the eaves. He had slept later than usual. One of the Lilley boys was ringing an ax vigorously at the woodpile. The smell of smoke assailed Dodge's nostrils. Sitting up, he threw off the blankets. The air was cold and frosty. Gold and red slants of light streaked through the forest under the wide porch roof. Evidently the sun had just peeped over the eastern rim. A wild turkey gobbled high up on the slope, and then the bugle of an elk came

down. The autumn morning gave Dodge a wonderful ex-
hilaration. But as he pulled on his boots he remembered
the menace that overshadowed the Lilleys. It seemed to
rouse a revulsion in him. The tranquillity and loneliness
and beauty of that forest land seemed a lie. Dodge shook
his head gloomily. The earth was wonderful and life was
good, but everywhere he had ridden, on the prairies, in
the cattle-range towns, among the hills, and under the
pines, there had always been and always would be weak,
greedy, and evil men. Perhaps they balanced life. Anyway, they had to be met and killed. Dodge came to an
estimate of his own worth without regret or bitterness.

He washed his face in the ice-cold spring water and
found himself tinglingly awake. Then he walked out to
have a look at the horses. He counted upward of a dozen
in the green lane between the cabin and the barn. He met
Steve carrying an armload of wood.

"Howdy, Dodge. D'je hear thet old turk gobblin' up on
the slope?"

"You bet I did. Gosh! I haven't been hunting for ten
years."

"Wal, it's a bit early fall yet. By the time we get all the
two-laigged varmints killed off it'll be about right," said
Steve. "Pack in some wood, Dodge."

When Dodge entered the wide porch between the
cabins he met one of the boys who struck him as looking
somewhat strange or unfamiliar.

"Mawnin', Panhandle," came the greeting in a voice he
certainly recognized.

"Nan! I'm a son of a gun! Didn't know you."

[127]

"No wonder. Reckon I'm just as tough-lookin' a hombre as Ruby Quayle," she replied.

"Ump-umm! You look like a real rider."

"Thanks, Dodge. I—I was afraid anyone could see a mile off I'm a girl."

She wore a gray blouse with a red scarf and blue jeans tucked into top boots. The high heels added some inches to her stature and helped the impression of a lithe form, but there was no doubt about her feminine grace and contour.

"Well, no one could tell so far as that. Gosh! I'm sure glad we're not liable to stack up against some of the boys I've ridden with."

"Why? Are you ashamed of me?"

"Nope. You look so darned pretty that you'd loco the whole outfit."

"Dodge, if those old riding pards of yours are anything like you, I'd just as lief not meet them."

"Now, Nan, what do you mean by that? They are a hard bunch, sure, but the finest fellows in the world— where a girl was concerned."

"That's why, cowboy. I'm fickle. Are you going to stand there all morning holding that wood?"

Breakfast appeared to be about as usual. The children were noisy and hungry. The boys stamped in and fell to eating as if in a hurry to get back to their chores. Evidently they were all used to Nan's riding garb, for there were no comments. Old Bill, however, did not manifest so lusty an appetite as on most mornings. He got up presently to go out. Soon Dodge and Steve joined him.

"What'll we do? Hang around an' wait for Coplace?" asked Steve impatiently.

"Son, you might as wal set down an' larn patience. Reckon this deal will last till the snow flies."

"Uncle, you're wrong. It won't last any time atall."

"How do you figger thet?"

"I'm figgerin' on Jim Coplace. None of us Lilleys but me ever savvied thet Indian. He always had it in for Hathaway. I didn't tell you. Hathaway had an eye for Jim's sister. For that matter, all the Ryeson boys had the same. But somehow Jim holds it most against Hathaway. Jim is no fool. He sees this deal of ours as his opportunity. You know some of the Apaches here are a no-good lot. An' it'd not do for him to kill a white man on his own account. But give him an excuse to fight, an' Lord Almighty, here's goin' to be a bloody mess."

"Wal, the sooner Coplace starts the better we'll like it," averred old Bill, wagging his head.

"You can gamble he'll start *today*," concluded Steve, with a rapt glow of conviction.

"Bill, I lean to Steve's argument," interposed Dodge.

"All right. Let's be ready to ride the moment Coplace comes, if he wants us to. Steve, fetch out yore dad's guns. Shells, too. We'll take stock. An' I'll set the wimmen to packin' saddlebags. We'll need a blanket each. Nights growin' cold now."

Proceedings of the next hour reminded Dodge of swift preparations of a posse of cowboys to take the trail of fleeing rustlers. To the youngsters it was apparently the sort of work they had seen often. Little Rock said, however, that he thought it too early in the fall for bear hunting. Steve handed over the newest forty-four Winchester and saddle sheath with the remark that if Dodge missed as seldom with it as his father had there would soon be considerable depopulation of the Tonto's undesirable inhabitants.

"Includin' bars an' cougars," added Uncle Bill facetiously.

Every little while Steve would leave off some task and stepping to the edge of the porch he would look up to see how high the sun had climbed.

"It's likely Jim would start long before daybreak. He ought to be here," he said finally.

Soon after this assertion one of the hounds barked.

"Ha! Moze!" exclaimed old Bill. "But he can't be trusted. Wait for Tige. Thar's a hound, Dodge. Nose like a fox. Ah-huh! Listen. Thet's Tige, shore as hell."

"I hear hawses," said Steve quietly.

Dodge was not a hunter with exquisitely attuned hearing, but he had the ears of a range man, and he seconded Steve's statement.

"Whar?" queried Bill.

Steve pointed down the lane toward the barns. "Cain't be Jim. He'll come short cut, up over the mesa."

"Probably our hawses," suggested the old Texan coolly.

"Dodge, cross the brook an' take a look along the lower fence. The trail comes in that way. An' keep out of sight. I'll take a peek down by the barns."

"Have a care, son," advised his uncle gruffly.

Steve strode off the porch and took to the side of the

lane, under the trees. Nan came out just as Dodge was about to leave.

"What is it?" she asked, her big eyes flashing.

"We heard horses, Nan. I'm going to have a look across the field," he replied.

Dodge leaped from stone to stone across the brook, and hurried through the thinning timber to the edge of the field. Then he peered out cautiously. Against the colorful background of the woods he could not distinguish anything moving. All along the wide-barred fence he gazed, to no avail. He listened as well. The September day was hot, still, smoky—a beginning of drowsy Indian summer. Suddenly a harsh laugh jarred his ear. It came from toward the barn. Dodge stepped to and fro, trying to peer through the forest. Trees and brush were too thick. Above and to the right of the barn rose a knoll of red rock, weathered into ledges upon which stunted cedars grew. Being the only prominent object in that direction, naturally it drew Dodge's gaze, while his busy and anxious mind considered probabilities. Then he sighted a man rise above a ledge at the back of this knoll. Stealthily he glided out of sight. From the cabin or the barns he could not have been seen. Dodge had caught a glimpse of sunlight on a rifle. He paused to deliberate. This man's action contrasted strikingly with the loud laugh previously heard and the hoofbeats of the horses. Some rider was careless while another man was stealthy. What did these circumstances signify?

Remembering Steve, he hurried back, aiming to reach the lane below the cabin. He lost a little time getting across the brook. Then rifle shots in rapid succession lent wings to his feet. He got out of the thick timber in time to see Steve gunning for the cabin. Blood streamed down his face. Shot, evidently, but not to the detriment of either legs or lungs. Dodge made sure the boy was being chased. Drawing his gun, Dodge kept to cover and soon peeped out behind the brush to look down the lane. Riderless horses were coming up. Then another rifle cracked, beyond the barns, and higher up, it seemed to Dodge. Instantly he associated this shot with the man he had seen stealthily climbing the far side of the bluff. Hoarse yells, then a volley of rifle shots low down, set Dodge to harder thinking. The lane toward the barns was empty of man or beast. Dodge turned to see Steve run up the porch steps to meet old Bill and the women, evidently badly frightened. Whereupon Dodge hurried under the trees up to the yard and the cabin, where, sheathing his gun, he called to reassure those on the porch, and climbed over the high rail.

Steve sat grimly loading a Winchester. Old Bill, gun in hands, crouched to peer down the lane.

"They're here, Dodge," he rasped.

Mrs. Lilley was endeavoring to crowd the scared children into the kitchen; Nan, with bloody hands, was wiping Steve's face with her scarf.

"Let me see, Nan," demanded Dodge, as he leaped to Steve's side.

"Oh, Dodge, I don't think it's bad," cried Nan.

"Hell no!" bawled Steve. "I cain't feel nothin'."

Dodge knew bullet wounds if he knew anything. He found a groove over Steve's temple.

"Close shave, boy. But a miss is as good as a mile. Get water, Nan, and clean linen. Wash and tie it up pronto."

With a cry of relief and gladness Nan rose from her knees and ran into the cabin. Dodge picked up the rifle assigned him, which he had leaned against the rail, and began to slide shells into the magazine.

"Mrs. Lilley, take the youngsters inside and make them lie down behind something," he went on. "Now, Steve, it's time to cool down. Tell me if you saw anybody and what come off."

CHAPTER 11

Steve finished loading the rifle, and bent over it with clutching hands while sweat and blood dripped off his face. Nan came running with water and bandages, to kneel beside him.

"Do it without coverin' my eyes, an' rustle," he panted.

Dodge was employing his keen sight to all possible advantage. Old Bill patrolled the porch from one point to another, crouching now and then to peer under the trees. The crack of a rifle at intervals and the whizz and thud of a bullet lent increasing excitement to the moment.

"Must come from the barn," remarked Bill. "All lead hittin' high. When they git the range of this porch, it won't be any too healthy here."

"They can't see the lower part of the cabin. But we'd better expect stray bullets," replied Dodge, glancing uneasily at Nan. Several of the giant pines in the yard stood in a line between her position and the direction from which the shots were fired.

"Lousy moonshiner!" bit out Nan. "He's no man. To shoot at our cabin full of children!"

"Steve, tell me what came off," asked Dodge.

"I'm so damned mad I cain't think," replied the lad. But it was manifest to Dodge that he was equally frightened.

"How far did you get down the lane before they shot at you?" queried Dodge, eager to have details.

"Clear to the gate."

"So far? An' then what'd you see?"

"Gang of riders—must have been a dozen. Some were out of their saddles, tying their hawses. I saw Hathaway—the —— —— ——! He was bareheaded an' his yellow hair stood up like a mane. Aw, if I'd only took my rifle. Too far for a six gun. Hathaway was pointin' around an' talkin' loud. Then closest to me was one of them Quayles, settin' his hawse, lookin'. He seen me first. 'That!' he yelled, an' tore at his rifle. All of a sudden he sort of quit. I swear I saw dust fly from his coat. Then he was fallin' when I heard a rifle crack, high up somewhere. Thet hombre had been shot clean through. My Gawd! An' you bet yore life I knew who did it. I turned an' ran for all I was worth up the lane, zigzaggin' from one side to the other. They began to shoot at me. Did I hear lead? Wal, I'd like to tell Dad I did, an' close to my head. I felt a burn over my ear. But thet was the only time they touched me."

"Ha! Luck's on our side," croaked old Bill. "But who'n hell bored thet Quayle hombre? You must be mistaken, son."

"Nix! I *saw* him stop—clutch his side—sag an' fall. An' I *know* the crack of the rifle thet did it."

"Coplace!"

"Shore."

"Wal, come to think about it, who else could it be? Boys, I'll bet—"

Spat! A bullet struck the wall of the cabin, under the porch roof.

"I seen thet one comin'. Thet's a sharpshooter off by the stone barn," called Uncle Bill from the far end of the porch.

"All right, Nan. That'll do. Rustle indoors," said Steve. "Whew! Listen to the yellin'. Strikes me all of thet shootin' ain't pointed this way. What you think, Dodge?"

"Steve, there's a little duel going on between Hathaway's outfit and our Apache pard, Coplace. I saw him climbing the back of the red knoll."

"No!"

"I did, Steve, plain as print. He must have beat them here."

Rifles were cracking rapidly now, and leaden missiles began to arrive unpleasantly close and noisy. Old Bill rested his rifle on the porch rail and took long and deliberate aim before he fired.

"Thar, consarn you," he growled fiercely, working the action of his rifle. "Boys, I stung one of 'em. I reckon some of them are behind the stone barn an' some back of the log barn. Them I seen acted damn fidgety."

Bullets continued to zip through the leaves and twigs of the trees, to spat into the cabin. They did not come in any considerable number, but Dodge found them worrisome. He was not used to this kind of encounter. Too much was left to chance. Whereupon he ran across the porch to get a look from Bill's angle. Through an aisle of the orchard he saw the stone barn from behind which rose puffs of smoke. Only the roof of the other barn could be discerned through the trees. Surveying the lay of the land, Dodge arrived at a decision.

"Steve, grab a box of shells and jump off the porch at your end," he called. "Slip down the brook and crawl up on them. I'll work off to the left, down through the brush. Coplace is holding them to cover down there. He might pick off a couple. If they rush the cabin—well, we'd clean 'em up. Bill, you watch from inside."

"Darn good idee. This is gettin' hot." Old Bill stamped into the larger cabin and stuck his rifle out of the window. Steve leaped off the porch and disappeared. While Dodge was hastily filling his pockets with shells a bullet of small caliber sang back. It ticked somewhere but did not thud. A cry of pain came from one of the children, then a scream from Nan.

"Nan!" cried Dodge, his heart sinking. He realized a bullet had gone through a chink between the logs.

"Oh, Dodge! Little Rock's been hit," frantically replied the girl. Dodge cursed in sudden hot rage and made as if to leap for the kitchen door. But that would not do.

"Is he—is he—Nan, don't say he's—"

"Oh, I don't know. I can't tell. It knocked him flat. He would stand up, peepin' out."

"Do your best, girl. Stop the blood," called Dodge stridently. "Denton, watch from the window. But don't make a mistake and shoot Steve or me. We're going to steal a march on the barns."

"Oh, Dodge, don't leave us here!" implored Nan, appearing at the door with white face and bloodstained hands.

"Nan, it's a fight," he replied sharply. "Get your nerve back. Use your wits. Coplace is down there. Steve has gone by the brook. I'll go through the brush. It's ten to one we'll drive them off."

Dodge hurried across the porch and bounded off to make for the line of young pines. Through these he stole swiftly but cautiously, making sure of his cover, listening for rifle shots. These had become desultory. Then they ceased. That might mean anything, but he took it as favorable. He came to the orchard fence and turned to the left, then changed his mind. The raspberry patch offered good cover but was too far off the lane. If Hathaway's outfit charged up the lane and through the thicket on either side he wanted to be near. At last he arrived at the corner of the pasture fence. Here was fairly good protection and a splendid vantage point to watch both the barns. He crawled into the corner and lay there peering over the lower rails. After a quick survey he swept the opposite side for sign of Steve. But there the jumble of rocks and patches of brush made the effort useless. Again he bent piercing eyes upon his objective. In the center of the wide space between the log barn and the corral under the red knoll stretched the body of a man lying face down, with that laxness Dodge understood too well. Beyond the barn, in a far corner, huddled a bunch of saddled horses, nervous and restive. Gradually they were working away from the vicinity of the barn. The stone

barn, over to the left, surely contained some of the be-
siegers.

Dodge's position was scarcely a hundred yards from the
log barn. He had an unobstructed view of all the ground
necessary for the enemy to cross, if they made a move to
charge the cabin. No doubt they dared not try making a
detour for fear the eagle-eyed Apache would see them.
Moreover, if Steve had found an equally safe and ad-
vantageous point, the Hathaway clan was in a tight pinch,
unless it lay low until night. And then moving out in the
moonlight would not be so safe. Dodge did not gauge
Hathaway as a man who had either patience or restraint.

At this juncture, straight across the open barnyard from
Dodge, puffed up a cloud of smoke. Crack! That was
Steve going into action. Dodge heard the bullet splinter
wood. An angry yell followed, and after that a furious
medley of voices in argument. Then a shot rang out from
the knoll. Dodge saw smoke rise from a clump of dwarf
pines. A hoarse bawl of pain stopped all the other tumult,
except the snorting and pounding of horses.

A volley was fired into the pines on the knoll which
did not worry Dodge. He knew the Apache would change
his position the moment he fired. Bullets spattered against
the stone wall behind the trees. Then Steve opened up
again. Bang! Bang! Twice more he shot in rapid succession, and the heavy bullets tore at the barn like a dull
ax on soft wood. Another howl went up. Steve had located
some of the hidden men. All this while Dodge had not
failed to sweep a quick eye back to the stone barn. He
heard shots and saw smoke. At length he saw a dark

aperture up under the eaves, where stones had been removed. Promptly he sent a leaden slug at that hole. It raised white dust and spanged off the rock.

"Hell's-fire! Snipe, we're surrounded!" yelled a stentorian voice of rage and alarm.

Dodge, recognizing that voice, turned loose his Winchester and fired a succession of shots into the hole under the roof. Evidently pandemonium followed the spang and ricochet of heavy lead bullets from the stone walls of the interior. Two men ran swiftly across the narrow space between the barns. Quickly as Dodge sent a shot after the second man, he was not fast enough, for the bullet kicked up dust behind. Then Dodge began to reload.

Suddenly something struck the fence rail above his head—a solid, splitting thump. Dodge rolled over and over to the left and hugged the ground. Some sharpshooter had seen his smoke. Cold sweat broke out all over him. His carelessness earned a savage rebuke. Was that thinking of Nan Lilley? Peeping under the heavy rail, he watched, expecting to see a puff of smoke come from the hole in the stone wall. But when the expected shot came there was no sign of smoke. That seemed strange to Dodge. A moment later a wispy cloud drifted on the air in range of Dodge's sight. It had undoubtedly come from a big cedar tree situated a few yards from the stone barn.

Dodge edged his rifle along the grass and cautiously over the rail. There was a man behind that cedar or up in the thick foliage. When he saw a puff of smoke burst from the foot of the tree, Dodge aligned his rifle on the spot. But before he could pull trigger a shot rang from the knoll. A threshing in the branches preceded the clink of a dropped rifle, after which a heavy body fell with a flop. Dodge, grim and hard, detected more movement in the branches. And when a lithe figure dropped into sight to bound up, Dodge was ready. With a swift shot he knocked this fellow down. Screeching, the man flopped like a crippled chicken behind the stone cabin.

In the ensuing silence a harsh voice pierced.

"Twitchell!" This came from the log barn.

"What you want?" came the curt answer from the stone cabin.

"We're surrounded."

"Aw, hell!"

"Thet damned Apache! He beat us out here!"

"Wal, I told you," called the cold-voiced, sarcastic Twitchell. "You wouldn't meet your man in the open. You had to start this backwoods fightin'. Buck, you got about as much chance as a snowball in hell."

"What'll we do?" raved the leader.

"What you want to do—fight or run?" came the scathing query.

Hathaway did not deign a reply. Dodge caught the sound of low, tense speech. Presently there followed a crash of an opening door, the thud of boots. Those in the log barn had made a break from the side unexposed to Steve and Coplace. Dodge saw dark forms flash under the cedars. Then one man dashed out of the stone cabin, to be followed swiftly by two others dragging a wounded man with them. The space between the barns was so narrow, the action so quick, that Dodge could not get a bead on any of them. But both Steve and Coplace began to fire again. Shrill yells, piercing whistles, the pound of hoofs, and cracking of dead brush—all these soon swelled into a concerted clatter of running horses.

Dodge jumped up to straddle the high rail fence, and leaped down to yell for Steve.

"Hi! Hi!" came the reply, on a wild and exultant note. Then Steve emerged from the brush and strode into the lane. "Come on, Dodge." He was bareheaded, dark and fierce of face.

"Go slow. Better call Coplace," replied Dodge, his eyes roving everywhere ahead.

"Hey, Jim!" yelled Steve.

An answering shout came from the knoll. It was followed by the appearance of Coplace on a ledge, rifle ready, his posture alert and suspicious.

"All their hosses gone, Jim," called Steve confidently.

Coplace waved a hand and started to descend the knoll. This was a signal for Dodge and Steve to proceed. They approached the man lying in the middle of the barnyard. He had been shot through the middle. Only half his face lay exposed—a lean, wolfish visage, ghastly to behold.

"One of the Quayles," said Steve. "But neither Ruby nor Diamond. I know them."

They waited for Coplace, but he did not join them. Instead, he went to the barn door and opened it. Dodge and Steve followed. The door had been splintered by bullets and on the inside there were bloody fingerprints. The exit of the Hathaway contingent had been through the back of the stalls, which opened into the corral. Dodge's experienced eyes noted three separate ragged lines made by the dragging boots of men hauled out to the horses. These lines converged at the corral gate, which swung open. Splotches of blood showed on the stones. Dodge trailed these telltale tracks out into the open and the edge of the woods. When he returned, Steve was going toward the stone cabin. Dodge strode after him, noting that Coplace did not join them.

"Here's another," called Steve, indicating the man Dodge had seen fall from the cedar tree. He lay like an empty sack. "Seen him somewheres," went on Steve. "Reckon he's one of Twitchell's outfit."

Coplace hailed them. "I'll get my horse."

"What'll we do with these bodies?" queried Dodge.

"Huh! Leave them to the buzzards," declared Steve. "If I know Jim, we'll be hittin' Hathaway's tracks while they're hot."

Steve removed the man's gun from his belt while Dodge picked up the rifle that lay near.

"Dodge, you bored this hombre," asserted Steve.

"No, by thunder, I had a bead on him up in the tree, when Coplace knocked him out. There was another man up this tree. He got down slick as a squirrel. But I crippled him."

They hurriedly retraced their steps, finding that Coplace had appropriated Quayle's gun and belt.

"Let's hurry," urged Steve.

"You run along, pard. I'll wrangle the horses. Better

brace yourself for a jolt. Little Rock was hit. Nan couldn't tell whether it was bad or not. But I reckon—bad."

"Aw, no!" panted Steve huskily, and broke into a run up the lane.

Dodge waited for Coplace at the junction where the west trail led off from the lane. Somberly he rolled a cigarette. He was used to the bloody business of fighting. But the peril to Nan and the injury to that bright little boy burdened his breast with leaden pangs. Hathaway and Twitchell would have to pay for this day's work with their lives. The Tonto was not wild enough to hide them.

Presently Coplace appeared leading his horse behind the saddle of which appeared a goodly pack wrapped in a slicker.

"Jim, you were there just right. How come?" said Dodge. "Did you trail them?"

"No. They was raisin' high jinks in town last night. An' I hung around. They rode to their camp late. When I went by at daybreak this mornin' they was gone. I beat them here by comin' across the mesa."

"How many in the outfit?"

"Nine or ten. Couldn't make a sure count."

"Say ten. Two down, an' three crippled that I'm sure of. Not so bad for a new clan in one morning."

"Had a snap shot at Hathaway. Missed, I'm glad. I want Steve to kill the —— —— ——!"

"Well, don't wait for that. I sure won't. Jim, I'm sorry to tell you, Steve's little brother Rock was shot."

Coplace shook his black head gloomily. "Too bad. Come, Dodge, let's start houndin' their tracks."

"Hathaway showed yellow, Jim. You should have heard Twitchell call him. To my mind that outfit won't stick together."

"Hathaway will have to stick. They'll hole in at his moonshine still, nurse their cripples, an' he'll fill them up on white mule again."

Dodge gathered that Coplace had verified his poor estimate of Hathaway's influence over men. He might rule by his liquor or by buying weak and vicious characters, but when actual fighting of a deadly nature set in he would turn out a hindrance.

Coplace went on up to the cabin while Dodge rounded up all the horses in the lane. Then he headed toward the porch steps. Old Bill stood waiting. Coplace was unpacking a bundle.

"Not so bad, huh?" queried the old Texan.

"How's the boy?" flashed Dodge.

"Wal, tolerable. It's a tossup. But I'll gamble Rock'll pull through."

Dodge strode up to look in the kitchen. Mrs. Lilley was there, pale but composed, busy over the stove. She had a smile of relief and hopefulness for him. Then Dodge crossed the porch aisle to the other cabin. Nan met him at the door. She had recovered, and appeared resolute and self-contained.

"Rock's resting easy, Dodge," she said, pointing to the white-faced lad on the bed. "I was scared wild."

"Where was he hit?" asked Dodge.

"Between the breast an' right shoulder. It was a spent bullet. I dug it out."

"Good! You are a doctor. I'm sure glad. Did you dress it well? Dirty bullets cause blood poisoning."

"No fear of that, Dodge, I soaked it with white mule!"

"I'll be darned. So that stuff is good for something. Nan, we're hitting Hathaway's trail pronto."

"Steve told me. I'm glad. My presence here means danger to Mother and the children so long as *he* lives."

"I've a hunch that won't be long," replied Dodge.

"Mother will feel safer if we're gone, she says. Denton will ride across the mesa to the Jones ranch and fetch one of the women, so I reckon we needn't worry about leavin' them here. But it'll be terrible not to know how little Rock makes out."

"Nan, it might have been worse. We drove them off. We've got them on the move, handicapped by cripples. It's the end of Hathaway, one way or another."

"Thank heaven! I have a feelin' that *he* shot little Rock. Here's the bullet. You see, it's not a forty-four."

Dodge studied the leaden missile. If he was not mistaken it had been fired from a Winchester thirty-eight. He handed it back to her.

"Someday we'll know."

"Dodge," called Steve from outside, "you an' Nan come out. Then we'll saddle an' hit the trail."

CHAPTER 12

Old Bill had the consideration to ride ahead and drag the gruesome body of Quayle aside among the rocks. But Dodge had a conviction that the sharp-eyed Lilley girl saw the performance. They need not have had any qualms about Nan. Her silence, her pale, resolute face, and the fact that she never looked back attested to her stern acceptance of a creed impossible to avoid.

Coplace rode ahead without a glance at the plowed-up earth where the hurried Hathaway outfit had taken to mettlesome and frightened horses. It was evident that the half-breed—noted as the best tracker as well as hunter in the Tonto—had never acquired the cowboy's habit of marking tracks from the saddle. Probably he saw at a swift glance what Dodge had to search for. The hoof tracks, cutting a wide swath, were noticeable for rods; but Dodge had to keenly scrutinize the earth to find spots of blood. It was his belief that the fugitives could not travel very fast or far with a number of badly injured companions. They had had little time to bandage wounds, therefore Dodge sustained a grim thrill of satisfaction when he saw scarlet drops on the shiny green manzanita leaves, red spots on the bleached logs along the trail, and wet stringy places in the dust.

The Lilley trail here was broad and deep cut in the soft earth. Though no wheel track had ever rolled over it— Rock Lilley would never have countenanced wagons on his homestead—it resembled a road more than a trail. And it led down through a forest of mixed pine, cedar, piñon, and juniper. Coplace led at a steady trot. If possible ambush occurred to him there was no indication of it. But he knew, as well as Dodge, that Hathaway would not soon wait to ambush a trail. Hathaway had seen men shot, perhaps had felt the score of a bullet himself, and he was all for flight. Scarcely conceivable was it that either Twitchell or the Quayles would remain behind to fight Hathaway's battle while he fled.

Soon the zigzag trail led down off the mesa. Dodge had a glimpse up at the magnificent promontory of the Rim, black and gold barred, red streaked and then terraced with green slopes and furrowed with autumn-hued canyons. The roar of the brook filled Dodge's ears. It had ceased its leisurely gliding, its reluctant eddying, and was now rushing down the valley toward that grim, stone-walled labyrinth visible from the ranch fields above. Here it was as amber-hued as some of the colored leaves. Sycamores, maples, willows, and birches shadowed the brook with a wonderful blending of yellow, bronze, purple, and red.

In the first flat of the narrow valley stood a rude log cabin, desolate in a squalid field of stock-trampled corn. A ragged, long-haired woman peered out of the door. A bristling hound barked. Coplace led on without apparent glance to right or left. Nan told Dodge that a settler named Hawkins had homesteaded the plot, and he might look upon the Hathaways with more favor than the Lilleys.

The riders crossed the brook, where the horses stood knee-deep in the cold, clear water and drank their fill. The dry rocks on the bank showed wet spots made by the first band of horses plunging across without being permitted to drink. The brook made wide turns and soon received the flow of a branch creek, after which it slowed up in deep, dark pools here and there under the big pines. Another log cabin showed under the trees without any garden or field adjacent. It was closed, a somber question in its one vacant window. Twice more Coplace crossed the brook and then took to a long lane under pines, where the brown pine needles lay thick. Here the guide loped his horse slowly up where the brook encroached again. Dodge had not ridden down as far as this, perhaps five miles or more from the Lilley home. He saw an opening under the trees, and soon rode out into a large clearing where smell of smoke and cabin roof and grazing cattle proved the presence of a backwoodsman. To the right of this ranch, at the brook, began the road in to Ryeson: twenty miles. The dust in that road had not been lately stirred by horses' hoofs. But the trail leading down the brook was dark and wet from the recent passage of horses.

"Wal, Dodge, here's the head of the Tonto trail," announced Bill. "An' it leads down into Hell Gate, whar we'll shore find our white-mule friends. Never was a sociable trail."

He followed Coplace into a narrow cut in the foliage. Nan was directed to go next, and Dodge fell in behind her with Steve bringing up the rear. The order of travel had markedly changed. It was single file now and at a walk. The brook entered a gorge and the trail followed it, up and down over rocky ridges, on the left bank. The shade was deep and cool; springs dripped off mossy cliffs; ferns drooped in the riders' faces; and ragged brush tore at the stirrups. The brook alternately roared and lulled, according to its acceleration.

At length the horses passed out of the covered trail into the open. Dodge sighted a widening valley, with a sloping mountain of pine on the west side, rising to a round dome, black with timber.

"Dead Hoss Hill," called Steve. "One of Dad's favorite bear dens."

On Dodge's left the slope was extremely rugged and precipitous, rising too high for him to see the summit. Evidently this trail and brook were the narrow approach to a valley, walled in by steep, lofty mountains.

So it turned out to be. One glance drew from Dodge an exclamation of delight and the words: "What a ranch, Nan! For us! If this country ever gets safe for Nan Lilley and her husband!"

"Bear Flat, Dodge," she explained. "It's wild and lonesome, even for you. Used to be Dad's. But it went to pay for white mule, I reckon."

"Hathaway's?" queried Dodge.

[150]

"So he says. But Dad never admitted that. No papers ever changed hands, I'm sure. Just little brown jugs."

"Ah-huh. Well, I'll give a thousand brown jugs for it, empty or full. Gosh, how pretty! There's a cabin under those big trees. Pines? No, they're spruces. And those patches of sumach on the bench, and the red vines—"

Dodge was surprised to find that Coplace had halted the train. He joined him and Bill while the two Lilleys whispered together.

"I saw horses. But reckon they aren't any we're looking for," explained Coplace.

"Four. Two bays, one white, and a sorrel," rejoined Dodge. "Men, there wasn't either a white or a red horse in Hathaway's bunch."

"They're making for Hell Gate," went on Coplace, with certitude. "I reckoned on that."

"Mebbe Bull Tank Canyon, Jim," said Steve, coming up. "Hathaway has some huntin' camp there. Often talked about it."

"Just a blind," responded the half-breed. "Steve, where'd you pack your sorghum down in here?"

"We used to take the road from Seligman's out about three miles below Dead Hoss, an' take a trail from there to the bare rock ridge west of the Tonto. We'd follow that till we'd reached the mouth of Bull Tank, comin' in across the Tonto, an' tumble the sorghum over the cliff. There we'd leave it. An' thet's all I know."

"A bare rock ridge," repeated Dodge. "Something to hide tracks, eh?"

"Hell of a five miles! We used to do up our hosses on every trip. Always went at night."

"Coplace, do you know the country?" asked Dodge.

"Used to do my deer and bear hunting here."

"Give me the lay of the land," went on Dodge. "I'm a range rider, you know, and I've been down on those Bald Ridges. I've seen where the canyons converge into one deep black hole."

"That's Hell Gate. Beyond there you have to swim your hoss. Hathaway may have his hidin' place there, but not his moonshine still."

"He'd hardly attempt to take severely wounded men past Hell Gate, would he?"

"No. I'm figgering the whole outfit will cross the creek below Bear Flat and make for friends over toward Green Valley or go on into Ryeson."

Whereupon Coplace dismounted to smooth a flat sandy place in the trail.

"Bend over here, you an' Steve," he went on, breaking a twig and beginning to draw with a skillful hand. "Bear Flat. Tonto Creek runs down, walled in. Ten miles down here, Hell Gate. Now up on the left is Mescal Ridge running same as the Tonto, till you get here—Bull Tank. Rough country beyond. Not for horses. Bear Flat road climbs up from here on the west side, crosses the foothills north of where the rocky ridges begin, an' goes down to the Green Valley road. About nine miles from up on top there to Green Valley. Homesteaders scattered all along. Getting populated beyond Green Valley. Some of these squatters must be under Hathaway's thumb. But not

Gordon. He's running the V bar outfit for Simpson. Nor is the new homesteader, Bailey, likely to be thick with Hathaway. He's clearing a farm, an' preaches all over on Sundays. Country parson. Hathaway might unload his cripples on Bailey."

"What would be Hathaway's object in riding down here unless he meant to hide in the canyons?" queried Dodge.

"His trail ought to tell that."

"You're right. His motive would be to save his own hide. Twitchell may want to fight. The Quayles probably want to get their wounded men where they can be cared for."

"Wal, I wouldn't be atall surprised if they'd split," put in old Bill.

Coplace's remounting his horse and riding on concluded that conference. No more was said during the brief ride down the flat to where it boxed in a great wall through which the Tonto cut its canyoned course. Three towering spruce trees, under which were the black-and-gray remains of campfires, marked where the trail led up to Mescal Ridge. No fresh horse tracks on that! Coplace found where the Hathaway outfit, complete, had crossed the creek to take the winding road up the west slope.

"What'll we do now?" queried Dodge, anxiously scanning the sunset-flushed sky.

"Rustle on," replied Steve savagely.

"Camp," contradicted the half-breed as he got off his horse. "I'll go after dark. Walk up, find them Injun style."

Dodge sensed a break in the strain at least for himself and Nan. As far as they were concerned the pursuit had ended for that day. For Dodge the presence of Nan had magnified his feelings exceedingly. Ordinarily a man hunt in the life of a range rider was all in the day's work. But Nan was precious. Nevertheless, he shared her opinion that peril to life and limb on the trail of the Hathaway clan was preferable to what she risked at home without protection.

"Let's go back up the flat. I know a good place to camp," said Steve.

The half-breed pointed up the trail and grunted his satisfaction at something.

"It's Tige," declared Nan. "He's trailing us."

The hound saw them and broke into a run, quickly reaching them.

"Hi there, you old bear chaser," called Steve. "Not goin' to be left out of this hunt! Funny we didn't think of Tige. He'll trail any track you put him on."

"You can bet no man or beast can slip up on us when we're sleeping," added Nan.

They got off their horses at a point above the cabin where a narrow cleft in the cliffs let a slender stream of sparkling water murmur among and over mossy stones. The gorge was choked with autumn-hued foliage, now burning gold and red in the sunset. The horses were unsaddled, hobbled, and turned loose.

"It's shore takin' a chance," said old Bill, wagging his gray head. "But what can we do? The hosses got to eat."

"If Hathaway wasn't head of this outfit we're tracking I'd say we shouldn't take the risk," replied Dodge.

"You keep the dog. I'll go track them," was Coplace's attitude toward that risk.

"We'll take our saddlebags an' blankets," suggested Steve, and led the way into the narrow gorge. Under the cliffs twilight appeared to have fallen. Presently, however, it lightened as the gorge turned and opened into a level-floored, steep-walled canyon.

"Runway for bears down into the flat. See the tracks," said Steve. "Come on, over here under the spruce."

Dodge observed that Coplace had not followed them. He made a mental reservation that the half-breed would locate Hathaway's halting place before many hours.

"It'll sure be cold sleeping out," remarked Nan thoughtfully. "I forgot my sheep coat. An' this here thin blanket!"

"Nan, we'll bunk together," suggested Steve. "Leastways you an' me an' Dodge. Uncle Bill snores like a bull stuck in the mud. All hands cuttin' spruce now."

Steve had a small ax and old Bill his big knife, with which they cut spruce boughs while Dodge and Nan arranged them on the ground, tips up. Soon they had a wide bed a foot or more high.

"One blanket under us an' two over'll be fine," said Steve. "I reckon I ought to sleep in the middle. Huh?"

A blank silence ensued. The occasion had been too serious for relaxation. Nan glanced dubiously from Steve to Dodge.

"I—I never have slept on the outside—yet," she replied finally, and suddenly blushed scarlet.

"Wal, you're my sister an' Dodge's sweetheart, an' mebbe the old women won't never hear about it," rejoined

Steve practically. "Now let's eat a bite. I fetched a coffee-pot an' two cups. Light a little fire, Dodge, while I unpack."

Dodge gathered spruce cones and broke off dead snags from the tree trunk. Nan strolled away in the dusk with Tige. Presently, at Steve's call, they gathered to sit around the little red fire to eat and take turns at a cup of coffee. Tige hunched beside Nan, watching her with solemn eyes. And while they ate night settled down like a mantle.

After the meal they sat silently around the dying embers of the fire. With action over for the day the more subjective thoughts and feelings about the nature of their job assailed them. Even Dodge felt the gravity of the situation. No rest, no peace, no unhaunted sleep, no pleasure or talk until certain men were dead!

Old Bill smoked out his pipe and knocking the ashes from the bowl said: "Wal, I ain't feelin' so easy. But I'll tell you-all somethin'. If that Apache wasn't on the trail out there, we'd have more cause to be troubled."

"But I wanted to go with him," declared Steve passionately.

"Shore, son, we-all appreciate yore feelin's. Only you're riled an' overeager. Better let Coplace do the scoutin'."

"But Hathaway is my meat," flashed Steve; and from this statement alone Dodge gathered that the young man would be impossible to restrain for long. Dodge cursed the complexity of the circumstances. He wanted to stand between Steve and catastrophe, but he was forced to think first of Nan. Some desperate chance might have to be taken before the issue was settled.

"I'm turnin' in, folks," said old Bill, and rose to go to his bed on the other side of the spruce. "Reckon you'd better do the same. Coplace is liable to rout us out any hour."

"Come, Nan," said Steve, rising. "Remember when you an' me an' Ben used to play babes in the woods?"

"Tuck her in, Steve," rejoined Dodge. "I'll smoke awhile yet."

When the others were in bed, a deep silence enveloped the canyon. Dodge sat smoking and watching the last of the fading red embers. His aggressive confidence of the fore part of the day had oozed out of him. Steve should not be permitted to rush madly upon Hathaway; Coplace should not have the whole burden laid upon him; Nan should not be risked at all. These three aspects of the case baffled Dodge with their adverse relations. Luck might be with them, as up at the ranch. Still Dodge was not one to rely upon luck. What he hoped for was that Hathaway and Twitchell would go back to Ryeson. Among the hangers-on at the saloon, drinking and gambling, they would present vastly less menace than out in this rocky wilderness, in company with the backwoodsmen Quayles.

"Dodge", called Nan softly, "I can't sleep. Are—Aren't you ever comin'?"

"Right this minute," replied Dodge contritely, and hurriedly went over to sit down on the bed. In the gloom he could just distinguish Nan's pale face above the blankets. Steve was wrapped in deep slumber. Dodge made a pillow of his coat, laid his rifle and gun close beside him, and pulling off his boots slipped gently under the blankets. Nan was so quiet that Dodge could hardly feel her presence. Suddenly he felt her stir, then the touch of her hand. She caught his hand and slipped hers into it.

"I'll be all right now," she whispered. "First night I ever laid out scared to death. But for that it'd be—nice."

"Ah, I know, girl, it's hell," replied Dodge huskily. "Don't weaken. Think of Ben and little Rock."

Dodge lay awake a long time. He knew when Nan finally fell asleep. Tige had crawled up on the foot of the bed to curl at Nan's feet. The night had grown cold. The leaves rustled, the insects chirped, the stream tinkled, the wind moaned up on the slopes. Dodge seemed to lose these sounds for periods. The hound roused him out of the last one. Gray dawn was at hand. Dodge heard a fire crackling. Coplace moved to and fro in the gray gloom. Dodge rolled out, pulled on his boots, and got up. Nan's curly head just peeped from under the blankets. Dodge awakened Steve and made for the fire. Old Bill came stooping under the low spruce branches.

"Mornin', Jim," spoke up Dodge, restraining his anxiety. The half-breed nodded. There was nothing to learn from scrutiny of his bronze face or somber eyes. Old Bill arrived, yawning, at the campfire a moment ahead of Steve, who came running, his hair disheveled, his eyes under a frowning brow.

"Pard, where'd he hole up?" demanded Steve fiercely.

"Can't say they're holed, Steve," returned the half-breed. "But they stopped for the night."

"Where?"

"Belmar's."

"Belmar's? So close? Thet's not three miles over the hill. Why'd he stop there?"

"Reckon it was far enough for gunshot riders. I tracked the hosses to Belmar's corral. Nine of them, eatin' sorghum fodder. All dark an' quiet at the cabin. I rustled back."

"Let's have some grub on the strength of that," suggested old Bill.

"What'll we do now?" demanded Steve.

"Who's Belmar?" queried Dodge as he vigorously combed his hair.

"Wal, if Belmar ain't an outlaw, it's shore because we haven't any law here," returned the Texan.

"Bad customer? What do you say, Jim?"

"It isn't helping us any that they're laying up at Belmar's."

"Have you any plan?"

"Yes. That outfit will sleep late," replied the half-breed. "We'll cross the creek an' work round through the woods, hold 'em up in the cabin by day, an' burn 'em out by night."

"Not so bad," declared Dodge quickly. "I'll call Nan. Let's eat pronto."

When Dodge knelt beside her bed, intending to give Nan a gentle shake, he answered to sudden impulse and kissed her instead. She awoke with his lips on hers.

"Oh-h!" she cried, as he drew away hastily. "I dreamed . . . Where am I? It's so cold and gray. Dodge!"

"Yes, I'm Dodge, and it's sure cold and gray," he replied. "Who else would dare to kiss you awake, young lady?"

She got up on her elbow, to see the half-breed and the others at the fire. "Coplace! Did he find them?"

"He did, Nan, and we've got hot stuff on our hands today. Roll out. Try a dash of this spring water."

Before clear daybreak had come the riders were crossing the flat. Deer grazed in the field. Coplace led them across the creek opposite to where the trail entered the little valley. Then he took a long slant up the steep wooded slope, coming out on top a mile or more upstream. The sun was not visible, but the great Rim Rock, which dominated the basin, stood up blazing as if on fire. The morning was keen and frosty; deer crashed the brush ahead of the riders; bluejays and squirrels gave noisy objection to this invasion of their quiet haunts; turkeys gobbled from a distant hill. Coplace led a devious way through the tangled undergrowth evidently seeking the easiest going. After a while the riders came to where this hilltop fell off into a green, rolling forest land which extended from the gray mesa to the bald ridges. Here and there widely separated columns of blue smoke rose lazily above the trees. In several places a dusty road could be seen.

"No smoke from Belmar's cabin," said Coplace, pointing.

Dodge caught a glimpse of a corner of brown field hedged in the green. Sycamore trees with their white bark and golden leaves indicated the presence of a watercourse. Coplace took to the descent of the slope. It did not require long travel. At the base the woods grew dense again. He rode into a tiny clearing, walled all around by green foliage, and dismounted.

"Get off," he said.

"Pretty snug place. How far from the road?" asked Dodge.

"Reckon little too close, if a horse nickers. But we can gamble no one will come from this side," replied the half-breed.

"It's the road that comes up out of Bear Flat," said Steve. "Safe place, shore. Nan, I reckon you ought to stay here."

"What do you think, Dodge?" she queried anxiously.

"You stand no chance of being hit by a bullet. But you might be discovered."

"I could hear anyone ridin' or walkin'."

"Wal, I'd advise her stayin'," interposed the old Texan. "Nan, you listen an' watch sharp. Tige will shore know if anyone's comin'."

Dodge found it an exceedingly hard question to decide.

"Fellows," he said soberly, "if I was running Hathaway's outfit there'd been a scout on top of this hill last night and this morning, watching our movements."

"Hathaway won't be stayin' long enough at Belmar's to watch us," said Steve. "Let's rustle."

The half-breed was not sanguine in his manner or tone as he gave his opinion. "Best we can do."

That settled further argument. He pulled his rifle from its saddle sheath and strode off. Bill and Steve made off behind him, while Dodge waited to say a parting word.

"Darling," he said, taking Nan in his arms, "be watchful—careful. If this was not *your* feud I wouldn't leave you for a minute."

"I'll be all right here. It's you who'll be in danger. Play Injun on them, Dodge."

"Play Injun yourself. I may come back after you, when I get the lay of the land." Releasing her and snatching his rifle, he slipped into the brush after the others.

They had not advanced far. Coplace had grown cautious. He kept behind trees and thickets, stealing slowly from one to the other, peering ahead, listening intently. Soon Dodge saw the road. When Coplace reached it he carefully studied it in each direction. The forest was still. Far off a woodpecker hammered on a dead tree. At length the half-breed crossed the road. After this he proceeded faster without stops, until he came to a place where the forest lightened. Through the trees Dodge saw a clearing.

"Dodge, you work in from here," directed Coplace. "You'll soon see the cabin. The corral where they have their horses is near the road, on the other side. We'll go on an' take stands not too far apart."

Coplace led the others away into the forest. Nothing had been said to Dodge about his procedure after he did crawl up within range of the cabin. He grimly supposed he was to shoot at any one of the Lilley enemies. To shoot at a man who was unaware of his presence galled Dodge. He had to remind himself of Nan and that this was Arizona clan warfare. Most certainly any of Hathaway's outfit would have cheerfully shot him in the back.

Left to himself, he listened a moment, and then made slow, silent way in the direction that had been assigned him. Every few steps he halted. As he neared the clearing he found that he was at the extreme right end. A line of sycamore trees indicated where the watercourse ran. He did not smell smoke. Horses and cows grazed in the clearing, which appeared to be mostly cornfield. He saw pigs. When he got up to a thick patch of cedars that had obstructed his view, he cautiously crawled through to the far edge. His objective had been attained. Two cabins stood within short rifle range. They were connected by a porch roof. Doors and windows were open. But there was no sound or sign of life. The inmates no doubt were asleep. Dodge stretched himself comfortably to wait and watch, particularly to listen. The corral Coplace had mentioned must have been out of sight behind the cabins. It could not, however, have been out of earshot.

Dodge had scarcely given himself over to intensive attention to the cabins when things began to happen in other directions. He heard the neigh of a horse and what he thought was a shout, and off in the woods the report of a rifle. After his first start he concluded that he should consider only the shout. He could not tell the direction from which it had come. Sounds in the forest were always deceiving.

Wild turkeys were put-put-put-putting off to his right somewhere near Nan's position. The snapping of twigs and knock of bone on wood attested to the wary movement of deer or elk. A flock of wood pigeons came whirring over his head, flying as if startled. But the sounds

Dodge had particularly attuned his ear for—the kick of a hoof against a fence, or trample of horses on hard ground, or a whinny or whistle—these were not forthcoming. It was next to impossible for nine mettlesome horses to be cooped up in a corral for any length of time without making some noise familiar to a range rider.

Half an hour passed. Dodge concluded that there were no horses in Belmar's corral. This, in conjunction with the deserted air of the cabins, inclined him to the opinion that the Hathaway outfit had gone. Dodge's first sensation was relief, on account of Nan. But that feeling was only short-lived.

Next to startle him was the ring of an iron horseshoe on rock, off to his right, on the road beyond Nan's hiding place. A chill ran down Dodge's spine. He had not liked this day's deal from the very start. There had not been a stone in the little level glade where Coplace had advised the tying of the horses. Dodge believed there was a rider on the road in that direction. He could see the road where it entered Belmar's clearing and passed along to the west. Dodge glued his eyes to the narrow aisle in the green wall, expecting to see a rider or perhaps more than one. But none came.

He grew worried. This forest-land game was new to him. He was a plainsman, not a backwoodsman. He had keen eyes, but he could not see through a wall of foliage. And he could not read the sounds of the forest.

Dodge was used to making quick decisions. He made one now albeit this was not his line of work. He decided to steal back toward Nan's hiding place and ascertain if all was well with her. For Dodge that was the paramount consideration. Therefore he took a last look at Belmar's cabin, then turned to crawl and worm his way back as cautiously as he had come. During his by-no-means-easy progress his ears recorded sounds that halted him momentarily, to listen breathlessly. Then he would go on again without being sure of what he had heard. At any rate, the woods seemed full of mysterious noises.

When he got far enough away from the clearing for safety he rose to his feet and glided from tree to tree. Suddenly a rifle cracked behind in the woods. Dodge actually ducked, he was so startled. He heard a heavy bullet strike wood with a loud spat. Either Steve or Bill had shot at a man, or perhaps in impatience had sent a leaden messenger to awake the supposed sleepers in the cabin. Dodge expected roars of surprise and anger, stamping of boots, and answering shots, but there were none.

Then he went on, finding it difficult to be sure of the way Coplace had led him in. Another sound then, uncertain of character, brought Dodge up transfixed and trembling. It resembled what might have been a cry suppressed in a scuffle in the brush. A rifle cracked off to the left, and it was followed by a distinct snorting and trampling of horses. With his heart leaping to his throat, Dodge wheeled to the left and ran.

He expected to emerge quickly upon the road. But he did not. Instead, he found that he was going downhill. He remembered a gradual slope from the glade down across the road. Halting, bewildered, he realized that he must have gotten turned around. Baffled, furious, he waited for another sound that might perhaps help him to get his location. The forest wilderness had grown oppressively silent. Dodge could not wait. He took to the slight upgrade and kept at it so long that he knew positively he was not proceeding toward the road. He turned at right angles, to stride in that direction for a while. Then he took off to the left. In vain! He was lost in the woods!

In a cold sweat, raging within, Dodge sat down on a log to try to compose himself and think. Riders of the open ranges seldom lost their bearings. They had distant landmarks to go by. On the other hand, Dodge knew that cowboys in the timbered ranges often lost their way. It was nothing out of the ordinary, but in his case, with Nan alone somewhere in the forest, it filled him with despair.

At length he reasoned out that in his first rush after the gunshot he had crossed the road. In places it had been grassy, little different from aisles and glades of the forest. In this case the thing for him to do was to take to the upgrade, climb to the hilltop, and locate his position. That would be easy if he happened to find the hill Coplace had descended, or if he crossed horse tracks.

The slope before him was steep and thickly overgrown with timber and brush besides being interminably long. When at last he surmounted it he found himself on top of one of many foothills all much alike. The green rolling descent, the columns of smoke, and stretches of road which he had noted when Coplace had halted that morning were not in sight. Nor the Bald Ridges! Looking the other way, however, he saw the magnificent Rim, and from its conformation and the promonotory he remembered he got his bearings.

Descending at a slant toward the east, he eventually came to the road. In dusty places he found numerous horse tracks all heading west. They were fresh, and on top of the impressions made early that morning. When it came to tracks Dodge might as well have had a printed page before him. Suddenly he recognized Baldy's hoof mark. He would have known it among a thousand.

"By jumpin' grasshoppers!" he soliloquized, aghast. "Baldy! My own horse. All our horses, easing along here. Coplace! And he was trailing."

That was how Dodge translated these tracks. He backtrailed them. Rounding a bend in the road, he was amazed to see the Belmar clearing ahead instead of behind him. He glided into the woods, made a detour back to the road, picked up the tracks again, and trailed them to where they came down out of the forest.

In a few more moments Dodge stood in the little forest-walled glade where Coplace had left the horses. He went carefully over all the ground without finding anything to excite interest. A quarrelsome squirrel, however, guided him to the base of a tree just outside the glade. Here he found a piece of greasy paper which undoubtedly had been around meat and biscuit. Nan had been there quite awhile. It was now late afternoon.

Dodge made a minute search of the trail down to the road. Under a juniper, where the ground was clean and brown, Dodge saw one of Nan's buckskin gloves. He snatched it up, suddenly going from hot to cold. Then his eyes fastened on the ground under that tree until he found other signs. Nan's small boot tracks—the imprints of her round knees close to the tree trunk, the sharp circular mark made by the butt of her rifle, and then, damnable ending, ground plowed up by a scuffle, in which a man's boot tracks cut deep.

CHAPTER 13

For a moment Dodge went cold and sick to the marrow of his bones. He did not delude himself with hopes. Some of Hathaway's backwoodsmen had been prowling by on foot, anticipating Coplace's move, and they had heard or seen Nan, to her undoing. Coplace, Steve, Bill, returning without him, had found Nan gone. Their conclusion would be, unless the half-breed had taken time to track things out—which he probably had not —that Dodge for reasons of safety had made off with Nan. Just why Coplace and the others had ridden down the road Dodge could not figure. It was possible, of course, that some of Hathaway's outfit had taken the horses as well as Nan. So Dodge worked it out, and likewise the only course he could pursue.

Whoever had Nan—and somehow Dodge inclined to the conviction that it was the Quayles—would avoid the road yet work on to where Hathaway would halt again. That would probably be at the cabin of another of his white-mule customers.

Dodge edged into the woods and hurried noiselessly

west, halting every fifty or more strides to peer out and listen. He moved into the woods to pass Belmar's homestead, then went on, at frequent intervals scrutinizing the road. A mile west of Belmar's he came upon three sets of foot-prints that stopped his heart. A bare patch of red ground, a little off the road, betrayed the truth Dodge had suspected. Nan's little boot imprints showed between those of two men, one on each side of her, and in places they had dragged her.

Sunset was at hand now. In his hurry Dodge passed a point where the fresher horse tracks left the road. He looked in vain for Baldy's track. But as he again found signs that Nan's captors had gone on with her, Dodge kept to that direction. Deep in the forest below the road he heard the bay of a hound. Then he remembered Tige. Had the hound stayed with Nan? Perhaps the shot Dodge had heard had silenced Tige.

Dodge strode on, growing bolder and swifter as twilight began to gloom the forest. He kept to the edge of the road. There would be another homestead presently, one Co-place had pointed out from the hilltop.

Darkness fell. Dodge thought that he had traveled at least five miles. He smelled smoke. Faint sounds broke the gloomy forest stillness. The evening star stood above the spear-pointed forest. A coyote wailed. Dodge realized that he was coming to the end of his frantic pursuit that night.

The road ascended a grade and turned abruptly down into a large clearing. Lights glimmered. And sounds of coarse revelry greeted Dodge's strained ears. This clearing had been recently cut. The fences were new. A long yellow cabin showed in the glare of a campfire. Dark figures of men crossed the light. This place had the pretentions of a ranch. Dodge halted for a moment. He did not need to see that Hathaway had stopped here. He heard the long, sonorous, wild laughter of the moonshiner. Hathaway was happy, for some reason, and it boded no good for Nan.

It looked to Dodge as if a barn and corral lay beyond the cabin. These furnished a background for the cheerful blaze. Closer scrutiny revealed that the long cabin consisted really of two sections under one roof with a wide porch between and also all along the front. This type of construction appeared to be the rule in that country. The end of the cabin closest to Dodge was dark. Beyond shone two bright lights.

Dodge had had more than enough to inflame him that day. He had burned with fury. Now his blood ran cold. He would give this Hathaway clan a taste of a range gunman's swift shooting. Dodge knew of a certainty that Coplace with his allies were hiding out there in the gloom or would be very soon. What he started they would finish, if he could not finish it himself. But Nan Lilley should not be left another moment at the mercy of Hathaway.

Advancing again, Dodge drew his gun. He had the rifle in his left hand. A shadow cast by the cabin hid his approach until he stepped up on the porch. Then a man in rough garb and high boots, standing in the light, saw Dodge and came to meet him.

"Thet you, Beezy? Buck's raisin' hell. Hyar!"

The man's intimate voice froze as Dodge swung the rifle. The blow catapulted him off the porch. Dodge took a stride forward, peered in at the first opening which was dark. But light came through a door into the second room of the cabin. He stepped in noiselessly, aware of voices.

"My dear young woman," a grave masculine voice was saying, "it's bad enough for me—but for you—monstrous if you have no love for this—"

"Love!" rang Nan's voice, trembling with passion. "Listen, I hate this moonshiner Hathaway. He shot my brother. He is responsible for the death of my father—perhaps my little brother. It's a bloody feud now between the Lilley and Hathaway clans. I'll kill him if I can. But he's got me now. These damned Quayles trailed me—caught me. Hathaway wants me. He can't see that I'd make away with myself before I'd give in. But anything to stall him off—to hold up his outfit! That's my game. My clan are on my trail. My man, Dodge Mercer, will never leave me a night in this Hathaway's hands."

"I see. But it's a sin for you to marry him," expostulated the other, who was manifestly the parson Bailey.

"Sin, yes. But if I *can't* kill him or myself before he forces me, it'd be better to be his wife, wouldn't it?"

"I don't see that, Miss Lilley. Under the circumstances I would have to refuse."

"We're wasting our breath. Hathaway will make you marry us. Or he'll shoot you. I tell you it'll help me fool him till—"

Dodge yielded to overmastering impulse. All the wild

career behind him flashed up to dominate the moment. He stepped to the door.

"Nan, don't scream, it's Dodge," he called, low and sharply.

She sustained a violent start but lost neither wit nor nerve. A rich color suffused her pale face and her eyes dilated.

"Oh, Dodge!" she cried. She manifestly restrained a desire to rush to him. Then she turned to the parson. "Mr. Bailey, this is Dodge Mercer."

"Howdy, Parson," said Dodge coolly as he surveyed the bearded Bailey, who stood frightened by this armed intruder.

"You came—in time, sir," he gulped. "That ungodly crew out there are drinking. Their chief means harm to this young woman. Take her away."

"He'd kill you, Parson, just like Nan said. There's a guard out front somewhere. Besides—"

Dodge peered out of the front window to see a man at the far end of the porch. He had not been there when Dodge came up. He appeared to be gazing toward the campfire, which Dodge could not see from this angle. Dodge leaped to the door leading out upon the porch between the cabins. From here he could see the bright fire and the men around it. The distance was perhaps a hundred feet. Seven men, one of them of huge stature, probably Belmar, another with an arm in a sling, one with a bandaged head, formed the circle around that blaze. Hathaway, standing in the light, his tawny hair

[173]

shining, appeared to be confronted by a man of slight stature but most forceful presence.

"I tell you that was a hell of a move—to shoot one of your own clan," he declared bitingly. Dodge recognized the vibrant voice. Snipe Twitchell!

"Wal, I ain't sayin' it wasn't," replied Hathaway doggedly.

"What for? I wasn't there. What'd you give Ruby Quayle that bad gunshot fer?"

"He insulted my girl."

"*What?*" hissed Twitchell, like a striking snake. "Who told you?"

"Nan. An' don't you hiss at me, Snipe Twitchell."

"So the girl told you, eh? An' suppose you tip us off?"

"She asked for my gun. Swore she'd do for Ruby. That was enough for me. I came here an' shot him myself. Haven't had time to ask Nan what he did."

Snipe Twitchell appeared the strongest personality in this clan, if he was not its nominal head. He turned to a dark-faced, buckskin-clad young man standing next to him.

"Diamond, I reckon you'd better come clean with the facts," went on Twitchell. "We've got off to a bad start. We've gotta get together. Ruby was your brother an' shore you're sore at Buck. But tell the truth."

"Wal, when we ketched the girl Ruby went off his head," replied Quayle. "He wanted to take her off in the woods. I had hell with him. I said we can't double-cross Buck thet way. Wal, we dragged her here, an' all the way Ruby kept huggin' an' kissin' her. I thought she'd tear him to pieces."

"Ahuh. Thanks, Diamond. You've settled it so far's I'm concerned. Are you goin' to stick with us now?"

"I reckon I'll take Ruby to Ryeson, if he doesn't croak."

"S'pose he croaks?"

"Wal, I haven't reckoned that far."

"Buck, you see there?" rasped Twitchell, wheeling to their leader.

"I don't give a damn. I'd shoot Ruby again, or Diamond, or anyone—*you*, Snipe Twitchell, if you got to pawin' Nan Lilley," declared Hathaway stridently.

"Ah-huh! The hell you would? Wal, I don't take kind to such talk. But bein' fair—an' if the honor of a girl who hates your guts means so much in your queer reckonin'—I gotta back you up an' stick to you."

"All right, Snipe. Thet's relievin' me. You worried me. Have a drink on it."

"No more fer me. Buck, I want to talk over what we'd better do."

"Let it ride. Tomorrow. I'm gettin' married tonight."

"My Gawd! Man alive, are you goin' to marry thet Lilley girl *hyar?*"

"Shore am. Lucky Buck!"

"You're goin' to force this parson to marry you?"

"Wal, if he ain't willin', I'll make him."

"But we gotta ride away from here pronto."

"Where to?"

"I'd say Hell Gate. An' hole up."

"Suits me. I'll take Nan."

"Hathaway, you can't take a woman with us into thet canyon."

"Snipe, we'll argue it out off by ourselves."

"All right, Buck," concluded Twitchell, with a harsh laugh. "Git crazy mad an' come arguin' with me while there's a Panhandle gunman an' Apache hunter on your trail."

Dodge drew back from the door, expelling the breath he had held. He stood so he could peek out the door at the campfire and see out the porch window as well.

"Parson, we've got a couple of minutes," said Dodge daringly. "Get your Bible. Nan, will you marry me?"

"Good heavens! Dodge!"

"Will you? Hurry. It's a wild idea. But maybe— Parson, come on."

"Yes, yes, if you'll take her and fly," replied Bailey.

Dodge seized Nan's hand and drew her close to him. The girl, dark of eye, fascinated, trembling all over, appeared irresistibly drawn despite the peril.

"When he comes in—an' sees you marrying me—then you'll kill him," she whispered.

Already Parson Bailey was reading the service, swiftly yet clearly. Dodge had leaned his rifle against the door but still held his gun. Hathaway and Twitchell stood apart from the group of men, deep in colloquy that evidently did not please the latter. Dodge answered the parson and Nan whispered her affirmative faintly. "Whom God hath joined together let no man put asunder," quavered Bailey.

"*Ah!* We beat him to it, darling," cried Dodge, in rapture. "Now!" Seizing his rifle, he took another look out of the window. The guard was still there. Dodge almost yielded to the impulse to take Nan and run for it, shooting the guard as he went out. But again a temptation too strong to combat held him. Then from the door he saw Hathaway approaching with another man. If it were Twitchell, the life of the Hathaway clan might be short.

"He's coming," whispered Dodge. "Nan, play up to him. Fool him! Pick your chance. Then run out either door. To the left. Down the road. Run fast. I'll catch you."

Dodge glided into the kitchen. It was dark except where the broad bar of light streamed in the doorway. He stood just out of it on the left.

Quick footfalls thudded on the porch between the cabins.

"Mac, have a look outside," said Hathaway. "I ain't trustin' either Beezy or Dare when the white stuff's flowin'."

With that Hathaway's steps sounded entering the cabin.

"Parson, do I have to take some shots at your boots?" he asked jeeringly.

"You need not resort to violence," replied Bailey nervously.

"Good! Well, Nan, are you goin' to marry me or not? Remember, I'll take you tonight with or without marryin'."

"Then, Buck, in that case, I will," replied Nan quite clearly.

"Oho! Come around, hey? Parson worked a little religion on you, I reckon. Damn you, girl! If I wasn't so crazy over you I'd be sorry."

"Yes, Buck, on one condition. That you let—me—off—tonight."

"Let you off nothin'! Gawd, Nan, I'm hungry for you."

"Give me time, Buck. You don't understand—a girl—"

"Parson, splice us pronto. The quicker the better for you. We're ridin' off at once."

Dodge stood there with bated breath. He seemed filled with fiendish glee. This backwoods lout imagined Nan would soon be his. Dodge stifled a force that bade him step to the door and end the farce. But he waited. Nan must have a chance to choose the best opportunity for her escape. Those guards outside worried Dodge.

"Buck, I used to—to like you—before—" said Nan, in a strange tone.

"Before all these fights?"

"No. Before you ruined us with your white mule."

"Wal, it's too late now," he went on. "If you'd listened to me once! Now, I'm gonna break you, Nan Lilley."

"Yeah? Buck, a poor broke filly doesn't drive well."

Again footfalls creaked on the board porch outside.

"Buck, Beezy is comin' out front. He's been up the road. Don't see Dare nowheres," called Mac. "I'll bet he's back at the fire, drinkin'."

"Go see," ordered Hathaway.

Mac stamped back between the two cabins. Dodge saw him pass the door.

"Wal, preacher, we got about five minutes. Hurry it up," drawled Hathaway, tapping the gun on his leg.

"Ha! Ha!" laughed Nan, in wild derision, almost hysterically.

"Hey, what you laughin' at? I said five mintues—"

"Like hell we have!" blazed Nan. Hathaway's tall form came within Dodge's vision. She had given him a sudden shove. *"Fool! Moonshiner!"*

She leaped for the door, gained it. Dodge might have shot Hathaway then, but Nan was still lined up with him.

"Hell!" screeched Hathaway, lunging after her. *"Stop her!"*

Dodge ran to the kitchen door. Nan flashed by, bounded off the porch, to vanish in the gloom of the road. Dodge heard a sudden crash, heavy footfalls, and hoarse shouts. He slid along the wall, gained the steps, and jumping down wheeled with gun extended.

"Here's Dare—his head all busted," bawled a voice above the others.

"What's come off? Beezy, stop the girl!" And a tall black-sombreroed man rushed out between the cabins. At Dodge's shot his energy changed, but not his momentum, for he rushed right on off the porch, to fall sheer, heavy as a log.

"Look out, Buck!" shrieked Beezy. "Keep back!"

Dodge had just a glimpse of Hathaway's tawny head, low down, moving a few inches out beyond the corner. He took a snap shot at it, and then suddenly alive to Beezy's blazing gun he fired once at the flash, and then darted away with all his speed down the pale road.

CHAPTER 14

Flashes and reports behind Dodge urged him to utmost speed. Bullets spanged along the gravelly road uncomfortably close. But soon he drew out of sight and range. The shouts died away and then the shots. He slowed up, breathless and hot.

Somewhere down this road Nan would be listening and watching for him. No fear of passing her! She would know he must be the first man to come running along. Still, as he trotted on, round the bend and down the hill, without being hailed by Nan, he began to fall prey again to dread that she had turned off into the woods or let him get by. Then he slowed to a walk.

Breathless, wringing wet, and as hot as fire—for once in his gunman career not sick and cold after a fray—he moved cautiously ahead, straining his eyes and ears.

A rustling on his right stopped him in his tracks. Big pines cast a dense shadow there.

"Nan!" he called, taking no chances of missing her.

"Here I am," came in poignant tones from the roadside.

[180]

"Where? Dark as—pitch," he panted, stepping off the road.

"I see you," she cried, and an instant later a shape darker than the shadow reached him.

"Dodge!" she whispered, clinging to him. "Are they after you?"

"Don't—know," he replied, struggling for breath. "Gosh! Haven't run like—that since I—was a boy. Let's get off the road, and listen."

She led him under the pines. Dodge leaned his rifle against a tree and took his scarf to wipe the sweat off his face.

"Oh did you—get hit?" she gasped.

"Nope. But I sure—heard some whistles. That fellow Beezy sent a bullet—between my shirt collar—and my neck. Feel the crease."

Nan felt his neck with tender fingers, and then slid them up and around to clasp close. She sank against him, shaking.

"Dodge—did you—kill him?" she whispered.

"Hathaway? No, curse my luck!" ejaculated Dodge, with grim passion. "When you shoved him, and jumped for the door, I had a chance to shoot, but was afraid I'd hit you. I ran out the kitchen door—saw you going by. Same time I heard a crash. Hathaway stumbled over something. That sure saved his life."

She lay against his breast in a silence more eloquent than words.

"Dear, luck is with us," he went on tenderly. "Oh, Nan, but I was near crazy."

"Not luck, but God," she said solemnly.

"Nan, how did those Quayles ever catch you?" he queried.

"Dodge, I think Coplace slipped up on those boys. They are as keen as foxes. After you left, Tige whined and sniffed the air. Either he wanted to follow Steve or he scented something. I couldn't keep him with me. After a little I heard a noise down by the road. I reckoned I could risk slipping down a ways. So I did. I saw Tige's tracks crossing the road. That relieved me. I started back and heard something close. I sank on my knees under a juniper and looked around where I reckoned the sound came from. Then it happened. I heard rustling, then swift steps—and they had me. One of them knocked up my rifle as I shot. The rest you know."

"So that's it. I wondered. None but a damn idiot would ever leave a girl alone in the woods. Too curious, too brave! I'll know better next time."

"Didn't it turn out good for you?" she asked archly.

"It did, Nan. But oh! What I went through till I found you!"

"Dodge, it's a sure bet our men tracked Hathaway's outfit to Parson Bailey's ranch."

"Yes. It's likely they think I sneaked away with you for some reason or other."

"That little skunk Twitchell—he's the one to look out for, Dodge," she replied earnestly. "He had the deal figgered. I heard him say that between his terrible temper and a white-faced girl, Hathaway's sense had gone. It

[182]

does seem that way. I reckon I'm loco, but I can't help being sorry Buck didn't come in just about after we—you—after the parson had—"

"Well, get it out, child," retorted Dodge. "I'd kind of liked that myself. Doggone! If this clan business was only over!"

"Oh, how happy I could be!"

"Nan, come to think about it, suppose you call me something."

"What?"

"Guess. It wouldn't be so sweet if I gave you a hint."

"Oh, something sweet."

"Yes. A name you never called me."

"Darling?"

"Ump-umm. You called me that before."

"Dearest?"

"Same."

"Sweetheart?"

"Pretty nice, but not just what I mean."

"Lover?"

"No."

"Dodge, I can't think of any more," she replied hesitatingly.

"Yes, you can. You must. It's something you couldn't ever have called me before."

She buried her face on his breast and whispered, "Husband?"

Dodge's rapture broke to a sharp clear cracking of Winchesters.

"There! The ball's opened, Nan. Our outfit dropping lead on that white-mule gang around the campfire."

"Oh, it must be!" cried Nan, starting up. "But why did it have to be just *then?*"

"Right you are, little wife." He clasped her in his arms, kissed her again and again. "But we've wasted time enough. Come. We'll work off the road and circle. Keep right behind me. I'm getting my cat's eyes now."

Rifle in hand, Dodge led the way into the forest. He felt his way, where the shade was so deep that he could not see. And the desultory gunfire enabled him to judge of a detour that would allow giving the Bailey ranch a wide berth. At times he stopped to listen and to assure himself that Nan kept at his heels. She did not speak, but whenever opportunity afforded she took his hand. They traveled out of heavy timber into a growth of cedar and piñon, open ground where the going was easy. From a ridge Dodge made out the clearing. Then he saw flashes of gunfire. Hathaway's men were wasting shots at the black shadows.

From this outlook Dodge also ascertained that Coplace, Steve, and Bill appeared to be together at one point, an elevation to the west of the ranch. They did not seem to be firing at random.

"Nan, we've located our men," declared Dodge exultantly. "Let's hurry. We can come up behind them, and call. If Hathaway's outfit stay put till after daybreak their goose is cooked."

"So'll mine be—if you don't slow up," panted Nan.

They had proceeded a hundred rods or more, going slowly down into thicker cover, when suddenly Nan tugged at Dodge to halt him.

"Dodge, I don't hear any more. It's quiet all of a sudden," she whispered.

"So it is. Reckon a lull. That happens in fights now and then. All loading up at once maybe."

"We've got plenty of time. Let's go up high again and listen."

Dodge thought this a good idea and took the first rise of ground they came to and picked a way among the cedars and thickets. Meanwhile, no more firing was heard. But Dodge's quick ear caught a sudden clatter of hoofs.

"You hear that? Horses," cried Nan.

"Sure do. Now what—"

"Running, too. Coming closer," said Nan, in alarm.

"Yes. But on the road. It must pass under this ridge. I'll bet Hathaway has quit."

They came out on a bare summit in time to hear the fast, rhythmic clatter of a bunch of horses, running at full speed, pass under the hill toward the west.

"Nan, Hathaway has showed yellow," declared Dodge excitedly. "If he was dead or crippled, Twitchell would carry on the fight. Quit, by gosh! That's the end of the Hathaway clan. Gone to Ryeson, the fox! He knows the people won't stand for any outfit shooting up the town."

"It can't *ever* be over so long as Hathaway lives. Not for Steve."

"Dear, I wasn't thinking of that. I mean Hathaway has

cracked. Lost his mad chase of you and his demand for your property. That means the clan feud is over. I'll gamble on it."

"Lights in Bailey's cabin again. They must be gone. How are we to find the rest of our outfit?"

"We'll go down across the road, up into that woods, and yell."

Soon they came to a stock trail, which led down to a point where the road left the clearing. From here they ascended an open slope to a line of timber. Here Dodge shouted for Steve. Instantly a hound barked, not so very far up in the woods.

"That's Tige," cried Nan joyfully.

Next came a halloo, which Dodge promptly answered.

"Who's thar?" shouted old Bill.

"Dodge and Nan."

"Wal, come an' show us."

The patter of light padded feet preceded the whine and then the bark of the hound. Tige leaped on Nan. Dodge led the way into the dark woods, called again to be answered, and after a few more minutes of feeling his way through brush and between trees he was halted.

"Close enough, Dodge. Who's with you?"

"Nan. No trick, Steve. Tige is with us. If there was anyone crowding us he'd let you know," rejoined Dodge.

"Thet's shore, Steve," called Uncle Bill.

Then presently Dodge and Nan emerged from the timber into the starlight on a rocky hill above the ranch.

"Wal, whar'n hell have you two been?" demanded the old Texan.

"Easy, old-timer. How about Hathaway?"

"Sloped. Left their dead—if there was any dead—an' shore their wounded."

"Sloped, eh? For Ryeson or Hell Gate? What does Coplace think?"

"Hell Gate is the other way, Dodge. It ain't hard to figger. Hathaway hadn't the sand to stand an' fight," replied the half-breed.

"Wal, let's go back where we left the hosses," suggested old Bill.

On the way down through the forest Dodge told briefly of his experience up until he found Nan with the parson. Here Nan took up the narrative, evidently thinking Dodge did not sufficiently do it justice, and told what had happened after Dodge had revealed himself in the cabin.

"Wal, I'll be doggoned!" ejaculated old Bill. "Haw! Haw! An' Dodge didn't kill thet lovesick moonshiner. My Gawd, I can't understand thet."

"It just happened," replied Dodge grimly.

"An' you're married!" exclaimed Steve incredulously.

"Unless I'm a locoed gent."

"Say, you're thet all right."

Old Bill clapped his hands in the darkness.

"Hey, I got it figgered. Don't you remember, after thet first shootin', which shore was when Dodge was gettin' away, how we heard Hathaway bellerin' like a bull? The parson told him. Thet's what."

"If he did, thet parson is dead right now," declared Steve.

"I'd say yes to that. But we can figure on Twitchell. He

would prevent murder of a country preacher," put in Dodge.

"Here are the hosses," called out Bill cheerily. "An' I'm recommendin' we have a fire an' eat a bite, then turn in. I'm dog-tired."

Around a bright fire the Lilley clan had rather a merry hour, considering the recent deadly action. But it was explained by the evident relief over the sudden departure of the enemy and the romance of Nan's marriage.

"Dodge, you take the cake," declared Steve, at last realizing the incredible. "You marry my sister with a gun in yore hand waitin' to bore the hombre who had the weddin' all fixed for himself."

"Wal, I call it slick. Damn sorry Buck didn't show up," said Bill.

"Nan, I wish you joy," said Steve warmly. "I reckon Dodge is a tolerable good fellar."

"Thanks, Steve. I'm sort of dazed. But if it's over, I'm happy."

"Shore you'll be happy." Then Steve turned to old Bill. "Say, Uncle, it wouldn't be just the thing for me to sleep with Nan an' Dodge tonight, would it—cold or no cold?"

"Wal, it ain't just regular," drawled old Bill dryly.

"Nan, you shore ain't wantin' it, are you?" asked Steve devilishly.

"Wantin' wha-at?" she faltered, her face as red as the fire.

"Thet I share my blanket with you an' Dodge tonight?"

"Why—of—of—course," replied Nan faintly.

Dodge threw a club at the grinning Steve.

"Shut up, or I'll make your wedding night one to freeze your gizzard."

"Wal, it ain't been such a goldarned pore day, considerin'," said old Bill. "Let's sleep on it an' figger tomorrow what to do."

CHAPTER 15

Morning disclosed the fact that Steve and his horse were missing.

"Gone after Hathaway!" ejaculated Dodge, aghast.

"Wal, what'd you expect?" queried Bill testily. "Seein' as you handy hunters an' gun slingers can't kill the moonshiner, Steve reckons he'll finish the job himself."

"Oh, Dodge!" cried Nan.

"Saddle up," ordered Dodge, stung by the rebuke and terror in Nan's eyes. "Bill, take Nan home. Coplace and I will beat Steve to Ryeson."

Before sunset that day Dodge and Coplace rode into Ryeson, taking the long way round to avoid probable ambush. They crossed the fields to the barn and corral where Tommy Barnes had taken care of Dodge's horse. Then they entered the lodging house from the back.

"Howdy, Barnes," spoke up Coplace to the shiftless-looking man who accosted them. "We'll want supper an' mebbe bed for the night."

"Aw, it's Jim Coplace," replied Barnes. "Didn't know you. An' who might this gun-totin' gent be?"

"Well, he might be King Fisher, only he isn't, which is a damn lucky thing for Ryesonites," replied the half-breed gruffly.

"Ha, ha!" returned the innkeeper dubiously.

"Anythin' goin' on in town?"

"Nope. Sorta dull day. Lots of folks in, though, an' I reckon it'll liven up tonight. Thar's a dance on, an' Jeff Timms is rafflin' off a lot of truck."

"Well, in that case we'll stay," said Coplace. "Come on, pard, let's set out in front and see what's doing."

He led the way out through the hall to a porch, which appeared to be well occupied with lounging men. At the end, however, there was a vacant bench.

The sun, about to set, had lost its heat but was still bright. There would still be an hour of daylight. Saddle horses, wagons, and buckboards lined each side of the wide square, and it needed only another glance around to verify Barnes' statement.

The half-breed did not sit down. He gave Dodge a meaningful glance and spoke for the benefit of the bystanders. "Well, pard, I'll mosey over an' have a drink before supper."

If anyone had observed him, however, it would have been noted that he did not cross the square, but went down the street to the corner. Dodge lost sight of him.

Presently the lad, Tommy, came out, eager and wideeyed, to see Dodge, whom he approached. But he was not going to bring undue attention upon Dodge, as was proved by his inquiry about horses to look after.

"We left ours at the barn, lad," replied Dodge. Then he winked at Tommy and flipped him a coin. "Run over and fetch me a cigar."

The boy ran across the square speedily but did not return at once, which presupposed that he was intelligent enough to translate Dodge's wink. He returned at length.

"Here you are, mister. Reckon it's more stogy than cigar," he said.

Thus they diverted the casual notice of bystanders, and presently Dodge whispered, "Is Buck Hathaway in town?"

"Yes, he's in Ryan's now, playin' cards," whispered Tommy. "At the back table near the back door. An', mister, I seen Steve Lilley, too, hangin' round the front door."

"Who's with Hathaway?"

"Three fellars, two from out of town. An' his pard Snipe Twitchell."

"Good! Thanks, Tom. Here's a dollar. Hang around in sight, so I can beckon if I want you."

The lad took the hint and moved away, pocketing his coin. Dodge stood up to lean back against the wall. In the main all he had needed to learn was that his man was in town. Twitchell's presence did not complicate matters. If they were together, Dodge would as soon face both as one. Almost instantly the old hard mood laid hold of him. What could keep Coplace so long? Dodge could not figure that out. If the half-breed did not return presently Dodge would go look for him. It bothered Dodge, for Coplace was the man to take a shot at Hathaway on his own account. Moments passed. Dodge glanced to and fro. Up the street, haltered to a tree, he saw a white, black-spotted horse that reminded him of Steve's. More visitors had arrived in a wagon. The girls were as gay as their raiment. Some leather-lunged mountaineer let out a loud guffaw. Timms' store across the square was crowded. Still Coplace did not show up. The sun sank, and Dodge was about to move when he saw the half-breed coming. Again he had crossed the street down at the far corner. Dodge liked his stride, the poise of his head. All was well. In a few moments the ugly business would be over. Coplace had an extraordinary gleam in his black eyes, like fire snapping specks of rust off coal.

"All set, Dodge," he said.

"Now, Coplace, what'd you do?" demanded Dodge.

"Well, when I saw Buck I just slipped up to the window and yelled."

"What'd you say?"

"I said, 'Buck, enjoy your last cards, for Steve trailed you to town.'"

"Not so bad. What'd Hathaway do?"

"He jerked up. 'Who'n hell was that?' But I mixed in the crowd. I spied on him then. Buck had been losin' at cards which always upsets him. He called for another game, but his hands shook. That little remark of mine had done its work. He couldn't play cards steady for looking at the front door of the saloon. Then he got up an' went to the door. He called to someone. He was pale with fury, and probably skeered."

"You think so?"

"Yep. And by heaven it's fitting he should be that now. Go on! Sure it'll be easy for you to throw a gun on him. Go on! Before you get over there he'll have started to worry."

"Coplace, for an Indian you're excited. You forget Snipe Twitchell. Tell me where he's sitting."

"Back to the back door. Go in that way. Buck will be straight across from Snipe, facing you."

"Suppose they show yellow?"

"Twitchell? Hell, no! But you might have to drive Hathaway to drawing."

"How'll I get around to the back door?"

"Cross below and go up that alley. You can't miss it 'cause the saloon is next to Timms' store. And you can look in there!"

"Come with me, and stand pat till I yell."

Dodge pulled his sombrero down over his eyes and strode off the porch, apparently seeing nothing, yet noticing everything. The whole issue now lay with the looks, the actions of Hathaway and his partner. He crossed the square, turned to the right, went up to the alley, and down that to the open yards at the back, with Coplace at his heels. He had estimated the strides he need take to place him in back of Timms' store. But the observation was not necessary, as he could see into the store from the back. Close to the corner of the adjoining building was an unlatched door, hand stained from long usage. Dodge shoved it open in a single sweep and entered.

His magnified sight grasped all but emphasized the table and figures in the foreground. Three men were sitting, one of whom, undersized and misshapen of head, was Snipe Twitchell.

"— in hell has got into you?" he was demanding shrilly.

Buck Hathaway stood just behind his empty chair, some cards in his hand. At sight of Dodge he gave an up-heaving start, then he froze.

Dodge took two long strides, and swinging his leg kicked the table so powerfully that cards, glasses, coins went flying to the ceiling while the table turned completely over to crash with Hathaway's empty chair to the floor. The undersized, bareheaded member of that quartet leaped up and forward, then wheeled. His action lined him up beside Hathaway. It had been ordered for Dodge.

"Don't move!" His ringing command, following the crash of table and chairs, silenced that crowded saloon.

Still Hathaway held to the cards. The quiver in his hand was noticeable even to Dodge, though he looked directly only at the eyes of the two men he faced. Dodge saw that Twitchell knew him.

"Who'n hell are you?" he demanded, nevertheless.

"By Gawd, Snipe, it's that Panhandle rider!" ejaculated Hathaway, and the false courage credited to his rage did not manifest itself here.

"Twitchell, you're one man I'm looking for," called out Dodge piercingly.

"That so?" Twitchell did not appear intimidated, nor even frightened, but he was dominated. He had not the swift-thinking brain of a gunman.

"We've met before, and not lately."

"Have we?"

"You know damn well we have."

"Wal, I shore don't recollect yore face."

"No. Because my face was turned away. *You shot me in the back!*"

To do Twitchell justice, he had courage. He might have denied the accusation, but manifestly he gathered that Dodge knew the truth and he was not the man to lie. His eyes emitted a greenish luster.

"Sho-ore," he replied, hoarse and slow, and his calculating was as plain to Dodge as writing on a wall. "I made a pore shot once—but next time—you Kansas—dodger—*now!*"

His twitching hand jerked down and back. By the time it reached his hip Dodge had thrown his gun and fired. Before Twitchell dropped, as if his legs had been chopped from under him, a blue hole appeared magically in the middle of his misshapen forehead.

Only one thing prevented Dodge from meting out the same fate to Hathaway, and that was a remarkable action, considering the moment. Hathaway raised the cards still in his right hand. Dodge cursed. He could not shoot the man under such circumstances.

"You lousy moonshiner!" Dodge yelled in a release of cold deliberation.

Hathaway, pallid and shaking, then threw down the cards. If he had been livid with rage, he was now pale. He recognized something that had been blank to him heretofore. Twitchell's head lay on his feet, and when Hathaway stepped back it thudded to the floor. But he had not glanced down.

[196]

"Get your gun out," ordered Dodge fiercely, stepping between the motionless gamblers and across Twitchell's body. "You've been free enough with it around lately."

"Wal, I ain't tryin' no even breaks with you," snarled Hathaway.

"You're a yellow-bellied coward," said Dodge furiously, and sheathing his gun he struck his opponent a sounding slap with his open right hand and then with his left fist, as once before, and floored him. Then Dodge, seeing his chance to kill the man fading away, gave way to fury. As Hathaway endeavored to rise to his hands and knees, Dodge placed a heavy boot to his rear and shoved him sprawling in the sawdust of the floor. The crowd spread and bellowed its approval. Hathaway tried to get up only to be again sent plowing through the dirt. A third attempt was no less futile, when Dodge quit and shouted after him.

"Gun or no gun—I'll shoot you—when I see you again!" panted Dodge.

Hathaway got up and ran out of the saloon. The scrape of boots and buzz of voices, now rising, were suddenly checked by a gunshot outside, then another so swiftly following it as to seem almost a continuation of the first. Dodge rushed out of the saloon, his gun leaping in his hand. Had that moonshiner run into Steve? In the passion of the moment he had forgotten the boy.

The space before the saloon was vacant, except for two figures, one erect, the other prostrate. Smoke drifted away. Bystanders gasped. There stood Steve Lilley, bareheaded, his hair erect, his eyes loosing a terrible glare, his arm stiff at his side. On the ground lay Buck Hathaway, flat on his back, a great bloody patch in the center of his white shirt, his body straining. It relaxed while Dodge stared, and his hand loosed its grip on his smoking gun.

"Wal, Kansas, it shore was the purtiest meetin' you ever seen," drawled someone from somewhere nearby. "Buck came rarin' out an' run plumb into Steve. Steve throwed his gun an' Buck drawed his. An' as the fool might have figgered he was bored before his gun went off."

CHAPTER 16

Coplace kept the growing crowd back while Dodge hurried to Steve's side and led him away toward the lodging house.

"Reckon you won't need your gun any more," said Dodge, as he exerted pressure on Steve's rigid arm.

"Was—he—dead?" panted the lad, in a hoarse whisper.

"He sure is by now," replied Dodge. "Croaking when I ran out."

"Oh, Gawd! But it—had to—be done."

Steve's face had lost its stiffness and was now convulsed. Dodge felt the break in his muscular rigidity. He shoved curious spectators aside with scant ceremony, and dragging Steve into the tavern, he spoke sharply to the awed and curious Barnes.

"Give us a room. And keep the crowd out."

Once inside the room Dodge relaxed his hold on Steve, who sagged on the bed.

"Steve, I know how you feel," said Dodge, without the sympathy his words implied. "Your guts have turned over on you. The thing to do is to fight that sickness. Suppose you had to meet Hathaway's pard right now! Think of Tess and Nan. Think how it'd break their hearts if you lay out in the street dead, instead of him. Think of Ben. Think that you did right. Fight it out. I'll lock you in here and wait outside till you call."

Dodge left the room. He locked the door and stood erect, his back to the wall. Supper was being set upon one of the tables for several men. There was an excited group out on the porch. Barnes stood at the door trying to keep people out. Youthful and weather-beaten and grizzled faces peeped in the door and the open window. Dodge knew he did not look particularly inviting at the moment. He tried not to distinguish what was being said. But presently, in the case of an outsider who accosted Barnes, that was impossible.

"Sam, ask that Kansas rider if I can speak to him."

"Wal, Simpson, I'll ask him, but it's yore risk," replied Barnes.

"Howdy, Simpson," spoke up a voice Dodge recognized. "Sure you can speak to him. Come in."

Whereupon Coplace entered with a sturdy man whose boots rang on the stone floor. He looked as though he belonged to pioneer stock and he had a blue flame in his eye. They advanced until the half-breed halted.

"Dodge, this is Simpson, cattleman across the valley."

"I'm in no mood to talk, sir," returned Dodge brusquely.

"Wal, you don't need to," replied Simpson heartily. "I'm drivin' home with my womenfolk, who're a little scared, an' I wanted a word with you."

Dodge knew the men it was always well to meet on an

equal footing, and he swallowed hard to get rid of his gorge and be courteous.

"Thanks, Mr. Simpson. I'll listen."

"Did you ever hear of Josh Turner, Abilene cowman?"

"I reckon. I rode for him for two years," rejoined Dodge quickly.

"Wal, Josh is related to me, an' if you needed any reference here, he'd shore do. But you don't need any. I just left a couple of the solid cattlemen around these parts an' we agreed thet we'd like a few more riders of yore breed. Is thet clear to you?"

"Yes, sir. I'm sure obliged," returned Dodge feelingly.

"Look me up sometime an' we'll talk cattle. Tell young Lilley thet he's a chip off the old block. Good day to you. An' you, Coplace."

"Good day, sir," said Dodge, while Coplace went to the door with the rancher. Presently he came back.

"Jim, that was sure decent of him. How can we take it?"

"You can take it as powerful friendly," declared the half-breed. " 'Pears to be what the whole town feels."

"No more of Hathaway's clan liable to be hunting Steve?"

"They sure vamoosed sudden," said Coplace. "Didn't see Quayle. How's Steve?"

"I'm waiting for him to call."

Evidently Steve heard these remarks through the door, for he asked them to come in. When Dodge opened the door, Steve stood facing them with flashing eyes.

"Well, pard, you're pale about the gills," drawled Dodge coolly.

"You both double-crossed me," burst out Steve.

Dodge interrupted the half-breed. "Let me do the talking, Coplace. Steve, we sure did double-cross you. Lay the blame on me. I'm as good as your brother already, and I can stand a hell of a lot. So cuss and rave. Get it out."

"Say, Dodge, I'd like to know how Steve figgers we double-crossed him?" queried Coplace, evidently hurt.

"Last night Nan tried to keep me from coming. She had a hunch."

"Did she? That's interesting."

"Dodge, I was lookin' in Ryan's door when you shot Snipe," declared Steve passionately.

"So you say, boy!" ejaculated Dodge.

"Yes, an' I seen you an' heard you brace Buck. An' I seen the crowd open up an' you kickin' Buck on his face. Mad as I was I thought quick to jump back out away from the door. An' I was standin' there when Buck bolted out."

"Steve, had you pulled your gun?" queried Dodge gravely.

"No. Never moved a finger till he rared up with a yelp an'—went—fer—his."

That relieved Dodge mightily. He remarked how circumstances might have gone less fortunately for Steve.

"I wanted to meet Buck face to face," Steve blurted out furiously. "I wanted to curse him before that crowd—to lay on him all the—the hell an' misery—about his white mule—an' kill him when he bellered! An' you spoiled it all! You an' Nan! Shore my bullet busted him, but he come runnin' out as if the devil was after him. A boy could have beat him to a gun then! All my foolin' an' practicin' fer nothin'!"

"Say, you're getting over it pretty quick, aren't you?" queried Dodge sarcastically.

"Gettin' over what?"

"Your bellyache."

"Aw, hell! I—I reckon I'm a little out of my head."

"I've seen older fellows do worse," declared Dodge. "Steve, do you want some advice?"

"Go ahead. I—I reckon I need some."

"Come with us and eat some supper. Then we'll go to bed and leave before sunup."

Nevertheless, despite their early start the trio did not reach the foothills until noon, and from there on, owing to Steve's varying moods, they halted in every likely spot. Finally Coplace turned off on the trail alone.

Soon after that Steve rode off into the woods. Dodge, glad to be alone, walked Baldy the remaining miles to the brook, and from there he lingered at every crossing. Under the pines, beside the swift-flowing water, Dodge gradually lost that haunting, mocking mood which was so bitter to realize. In the past, some hot, strong drinks, the excitement of the gaming table, or the violence of a long ride back to the range had sufficed to bring about his balance. But here, after a deadly fray, in which Nan's best-beloved brother had been involved, he could not hurry back to her. He should have ridden posthaste.

As it was he reached the ranch late, and turning Baldy into the pasture, he walked wearily up the trail. How

[203]

much harder the ordeal now than that of yesterday! When he saw white-clad girls on the porch he braced a little.

This was Sunday, always a company day for the Lilleys. As Dodge mounted the steps he saw Steve dressed in his best suit, clean-shaven, cool and dark as ever, somehow a man now where as he had been a boy before. That was a shock for Dodge. He braced himself further for perhaps a greater one.

Little Rock sat in a chair at the head of the steps where the other youngsters greeted Dodge vociferously. Uncle Bill, who was talking to a man with a familiar look, like-wise had made himself presentable. There were some new faces, too. Then Dodge saw Tess, whose pretty face matched the hue of her white dress and whose eyes were almost black.

"Dodge, what made you so late?" called out Steve, and he drew Tess with him across the porch to meet Dodge, where he spoke low. "All up, old man. Tess heard about it last night, an' no less than three fellars rode out this mawnin' with the news."

"Nan?" whispered Dodge.

"She most eat me alive an' she shore will you."

"Yes, she will," replied Dodge weakly.

Tess put a hand, fingers spread, on Dodge's breast. She seemed to radiate all that Dodge had felt in the forest. "Nan will—an' so will I. Wait!"

That, added to the dragging youngsters, made it about time for Dodge to sit down. It was good for him to play with the children a few minutes, especially to hold little Rock's responsive hand. But for him their future would have loomed black. So long as women dared the frontier, so long as children followed, just so long would there be need for men like him. But where was Nan?

Uncle Bill sauntered over with his companion, who turned out to be Tess's father. They sat down with Dodge.

"I've been talkin' about our deal to Williams," began Bill, "an' he reckons it good."

"Yes, the range is here, enough for more stock than we can ever breed," added Williams. "You see, Mercer, what's always been lackin' here was—wal, let's say an iron hand."

"Ahuh," replied Dodge dreamily. Had he heard Nan's light step?

"Thanks to you, we can settle down to ranchin', farmin', marryin', an' so forth. I shore congratulate you, Mercer."

"Me! What on earth for?"

"Listen to him, Lilley. Wal, the fact is, Nan told us at dinner."

"Told—you—what?" gasped Dodge.

"Shore it was short an' sweet about yore marryin' an' that. Now all yore trouble is over."

The pines and the hills and the sunset whirled around Dodge.

"Wal, to go on, I'll drive in a thousand head for Tess an' Steve as a weddin' present," continued Williams practically. "An', Dodge, if you want five hundred head I'll send them, rock-bottom price, an' wait for the money."

"Take you up," Dodge got out.

"Wal, when all these Lilley festivities are over, I'll run down to Texas hell-bent for election, an' git back the same way. An' you bet I'll throw a herd of cattle on this range."

"Dodge," called a sweet voice that made Dodge wince. "I saved some dinner for you. Come an' get it."

He turned to see Nan carrying a wooden tray toward his bed on the corner of the porch, as she had done so often when he lay wounded. Dodge excused himself and hurried to her side, and sitting down upon his couch he tried to force easy speech. "Howdy, Nan."

Not until she sat down opposite him could he see her face. It appeared to have lost something and gained more. The thought came to him that in repose it had always been sad. She was dressed in her best, and as he gazed at her his heart seemed to lift in his breast.

"Dodge, I sure didn't expect you to look gay," she said earnestly. "But as you came up the steps, I hardly knew you."

"Ahuh. Nan, it was ugly business," he rejoined somberly. "The worst was when I heard shots outside of Ryan's. I reckoned Hathaway had done for Steve. I withered all up inside."

"You *pore* gentle boy!" she replied mockingly. "As if *you* know what agony is!"

"Don't rub it in. I'd like heaps to have some days pass quick. What did Steve say?"

"Heavens! What didn't he *do*? I was half dressed when he came raving into my room with fire in his eye. And before I guessed what he was up to he grabbed me up like a jackknife and smacked me so hard I hadn't breath to scream. Mad? I was so mad I near died. But I was plumb scared, too. He dropped me on the floor and said, cool as a cucumber: 'Nan, you an' your husband double-crossed me. An' I'm head of this Lilley outfit. Do you savvy that?"

"Smacked you!" ejaculated Dodge, in amazed rage. "Well, if he doesn't beat the Dutch! I'll take a smack at him."

"Please don't. I deserved it, an' after I got over my mad, I was tickled. Tess was in my room. He never saw her. I told Steve I savvied an' he went out. Then Tess was funny. She never thought what that smackin' did to me. She only gasped: 'My Gawd, will he ever do thet to *me?* An' I bet he would."

"Young ruffian!" growled Dodge. "Did he hurt you, Nan?"

"Hurt! Did you ever look at one of Steve's hands? It's not a hand—it's a ham. Honest. I haven't sat down since."

"Ahuh. The way you tell this makes me figure that you think it'll tickle me."

"Doesn't it?" she asked, almost demurely. Then he divined that she was endeavoring to hide her real feelings, to get back her equilibrium.

"Not yet. Maybe it will—later. Say, look at the dinner you saved me! Nan, it was sure good of you. But do you think I can eat now?"

"I can persuade you to."

"How?"

"Oh, I can bribe you," she said, with a brave little smile. "I forget."

"About—about Steve's boast that I'd eat you alive."

"You must have been eavesdropping."

"Just what is this eating alive, anyway?"

"It's common talk in the valley between sweethearts."

"Ahuh. But what's talk?"

She blushed scarlet. "I'm not bluffing, Dodge."

"Doggone you! I'll call you, anyhow," he declared, and set doggedly to the task of devouring that meal. He discovered an appetite, which grew and grew until the last scrap of food and the last drink were gone.

"There you are, Mrs. Mercer," he said, with bravado.

"Wal, Mister Dodge, suppose you do somethin'," Nan said, resorting to the familiar backwoods talk. "Shave yore dirty grim face, put on a Sunday shirt an' scarf while I see our company off. After they're gone, we'll walk out in the woods to our green hidin' place by the brook where we met."

"Nan, you've got me buffaloed," he retorted dubiously.

"What's buffaloed?"

"All bluffed, scared, running in a circle. You backwoods Lilleys are a new breed to me. I just can't figure any of you."

"I'm as shallow an' easy to see through as our brook. Go along with you now."

The forest was still and cool. Squirrels were dropping pine cones. There was no breeze stirring to rustle through the treetops, but the stream murmured low. Scarlet and gold vied with the green foliage.

Nan did not break the silence until they were halted by the brook. "Come. We can cross on any steppingstones." And she led him along the shore to where a ledge reached halfway across and two flat dry stones made the remainder easy.

"I should have waded to you—as I did that day," Nan said pensively.

"Why?" he queried, curiously pleased with her sentiment.

She did not give him any satisfaction about that. Soon they had penetrated the leafy bower, strangely more beautiful to Dodge by reason of the purple and red leaves that had fallen on the rocks and the gold ones above which shed a glow of the westering sun. The leaves rustled under their feet.

"Say, Nan, I'd love this nook if you hadn't been here with other sweethearts," he said jealously.

"Dodge, I never had any sweetheart but you," she replied solemnly.

Instead of sitting down beside him, as he expected, she sank on her knees and leaned with face upturned to him.

"Dodge, are you glad you married me?" she asked tremulously.

"Why, Nan! Such a question."

"You'll take care of me, an' help me with little Rock an' Rill?"

"Bless your heart! As if I didn't thank heaven for the chance!"

The mask seemed off her soul then, and through her eyes he saw what made him reverent and grateful to the depths of his being. She put her arms around his neck and laid her face on his breast.

"I never understood about backwoods people an' ways till I went to Texas," she said. "I learned a lot besides schooling. But when I came home I didn't love it all any the less. Only I saw! An', Dodge, since the very day I came back till this minute I never drew a happy breath. I'm happy now—in spite of Dad—an' Ben. Something terrible had to come before things could get better. Well, it's past. I love this wild country. I love my people. I want to live an' work here."

"So do I, Nan," he returned, in swift tenderness. "Don't have a single fear of me."

"You're satisfied to have a backwoods girl for a wife?"

"Yes. And am I not a Kansas cowhand?"

She uttered a laugh that was half a happy sob. "So—you—say. But you—can't fool me—Dodge Mercer. You're a knight like that Sir Galahad."

"Knight! That means a fellow who's some punkins on a horse, doesn't it?"

"Don't—make—fun. I—I *love* you!"

"So you've said."

"Oh, I love you. But that is nothin'. I want to feel you—to know you're here—that I am safe—safe in your arms."

"Honey, you're in them, all right, and I reckon safe enough," he replied, bending over her.

Nan broke down then and wept. Dodge was stricken. He did not know what to do, but finally sensed there was nothing except to hold her. His mood grew serious, then, and as Nan gave way to uncontrollable sobs he began to get a glimmering of what the situation there had been from her side. She was more than a simple-hearted, strong, and loving girl. Life had been real and acute for her and the future black to contemplate. At length the paroxysm wore itself out and she recovered.

"Nan, I'm only a thick-headed man," declared Dodge. "I don't know anything. But honest, I'd almost rather have had you cry that way than—than have you do what we came out for."

"Wal, Dodge, I shore had to cry it out before I could think of makin' love. An' now, Dodge, I reckon it's about time for me to make good Steve's brag."